Sisters Under the

Also in the *X Libris* series:

Back in Charge	Mariah Greene
The Discipline of Pearls	Susan Swann
Hotel Aphrodisia	Dorothy Starr
Arousing Anna	Nina Sheridan
Playing the Game	Selina Seymour
The Women's Club	Vanessa Davies
A Slave to His Kiss	Anastasia Dubois
Saturnalia	Zara Devereux
Shopping Around	Mariah Greene
Dares	Roxanne Morgan
Dark Secret	Marina Anderson
Inspiration	Stephanie Ash
Rejuvenating Julia	Nina Sheridan
The Ritual of Pearls	Susan Swann
Midnight Starr	Dorothy Starr
The Pleasure Principle	Emma Allan
Velvet Touch	Zara Devereux
Acting it Out	Vanessa Davies
The Gambler	Tallulah Sharpe
Musical Affairs	Stephanie Ash
Sleeping Partner	Mariah Greene
Eternal Kiss	Anastasia Dubois
Forbidden Desires	Marina Anderson
Pleasuring Pamela	Nina Sheridan
Letting Go	Cathy Hunter
Two Women	Emma Allan
Blue Notes	Stephanie Ash

Sisters Under the Skin

Vanessa Davies

X
LIBRIS

An *X Libris* Book

First published by X Libris in 1996

All characters in this publication are fictitious and any resemblance to real persons, living or dead, is purely coincidental.

A CIP catalogue record for this book is available from the British Library.

ISBN 0 7515 1823 9

Photoset in North Wales by
Derek Doyle & Associates, Mold, Clwyd
Printed and bound in Great Britain by
Clays Ltd, St Ives plc

X Libris
A Division of
Little, Brown and Company (UK)
Brettenham House
Lancaster Place
London WC2E 7EN

Chapter One

LOUISE ANDREWS WAS lying alone in the wide bed, her eyes closed but her ears fearfully alert. She was waiting for the tell-tale sound of a key turning in a lock, the sound she had come to dread over the past few months.

'How often have you lain here like this?' a voice in her head enquired.

'Far too often,' came the sardonic reply.

Louise sighed and switched on the bedside lamp. The clock said almost midnight, so the pubs would be closed. That meant Martin would be home soon. She shuddered at the thought of him lumbering into the bedroom, reeking sourly of whisky. If he tried to kiss or paw her she would slap his face.

As if she didn't have enough to worry about already. The letter from the building society had come that morning, threatening repossession of their house. Anger rose in her as she remembered how hard she had worked to pay the mortgage. But she couldn't do it alone. And now her husband was both unwilling and unable to spend his remaining money on anything but drink.

Suddenly Louise heard the sound that chilled her heart. Putting out the light she huddled down under the duvet, hoping to convince Martin that she was asleep. She heard the familiar bang of the front door and the soft swish of his jacket as he let it drop to the floor, followed by the dull thud of his footsteps as they came straight towards the bedroom. He coughed and cursed, then flung open the door and flicked on the light-switch.

'Don't pretend you're asleep!' he snarled, pulling the cover right off her so that she lay naked and exposed to the glare.

Louise shielded her eyes with her hand and pulled the duvet back to her waist. 'Leave me alone. I'm tired!' she murmured, trying not to antagonise him.

His dark, drink-bloated face loomed over her, eyes red and cloudy, mouth contorted and emitting a draught of whisky breath. 'I'm tired too. Tired of being given the brush-off. You're my wife, Louise, and I've a right to my conj . . . to my connub. . . to screw you whenever I feel like it!'

'You're drunk,' she accused him. 'And I'm exhausted. I'm going to sleep in the spare room.'

She swung her legs over the side of the bed and rose unsteadily, but he grabbed her wrist and forced her back down onto the mattress. 'Sleep in there if you like, but first we're going to make love, my sweet.'

He was slurring his speech, and somehow that got on her nerves more than his clumsy movements or foul breath. Louise just wanted to get away from him, but she knew he could turn even nastier when he was in that state. As far as her befuddled mind could make out she had three choices: to make an escape bid and barricade herself in the spare room, to face up to him and risk a violent confrontation, or to give in for the sake of peace and quiet.

Wearily she settled for the last option. At least it would be over soon and then, perhaps, she could slip off to the other bed and get some sleep away from his loud snores.

'That's better!' he grinned, seeing her lie back and look up at him in submission. He took off his shoes, undid his belt and pulled off his jeans. She could see his prick rearing aggressively in his pants. Wherever did the idea that alcohol made men impotent come from? With Martin it had the reverse effect, making him more randy than ever.

The bedsprings groaned, protesting on her behalf, as he knelt over her and thrust his forefinger between her thighs. 'Just testing the water,' she imagined him saying in his usual vulgar way, although he hadn't uttered a word.

Despite her silent anger Louise felt herself opening up to him, yielding to his intruding finger out of sheer habit. His mouth was slobbering over her breasts now, making her nipples stiff and tingly. She looked down and saw his stubby penis rearing with impatience, then felt it knocking against the hard nub of her clitoris as he made several attempts to guide it into her. To think that I once enjoyed this, she thought.

While he thrust back and forth she tried to relax, even to feign pleasure, but all the time she was wishing it was over. A part of her was deeply sad that she was no longer in love with her husband, that she had lost all hope of ever recovering those rapturous feelings she'd once had for him. Her body still remembered, though. The reflexes that signalled her arousal were all there: her breasts taut and hard-nippled, her clitoris engorged and throbbing. It was a weird feeling, being betrayed by her own flesh.

At last he spurted inside her with a loud groan, then rolled off her and straight into oblivion. Louise lay there inert for several minutes, afraid of rousing him. She felt the juices dribble out of her and slowly her body returned to normal, the swollen tissues ceasing to throb. Beneath her fatigue remained a dull anger, twinned with hopeless despair. What on earth was she going to do? Clearly she couldn't stay with him. Not when their marriage was such a travesty. But where could she go?

Into the spare room, right now. Already Martin was working up to one of his snoring marathons and there would be no peace for her that night if she stayed beside him. Slowly Louise slipped off the bed and padded out of the room, closing the door behind her.

But once she was in the tiny boxroom that served as a guest bedroom sleep evaded her. It wouldn't be long before they lost the house, and then what? Although Martin still had his job, Louise was unsure what her own future held since the company she worked for had recently been taken over and there were rumours of redundancies. Just how much more could she take?

If only some escape route could be found, some way of chucking everything in and starting all over again. Louise knew that was wishful thinking. Even if they gave up the house she would still have her share of the debt to pay off. Eventually her financial worries would be over, but that left the far more important matter of her marriage. It was over in all but name, she knew that. But did she have the guts to face a divorce, on top of everything else?

Then she thought of Gina, and the germ of a plan began to grow in her mind. Gina was her half-sister, the daughter of their mother's first husband, and they had shared a stormy ten years of childhood, culminating in the older girl running away from home at sixteen. After that Louise had only heard from her sister sporadically, but six months ago she had seen a photograph of her in the evening paper.

Straining to recall the details, Louise summoned up a mental picture of Gina on the arm of some wealthy-looking Arab, which hadn't surprised her in the least. Now she remembered that the pair of them had opened some kind of club in the West End that had sounded a bit sleazy. While many of the details remained vague, making Louise wish that she had kept the article, she thought she remembered the name of the club: *Seventh Veil*, that was it.

Out of curiosity Louise crept down to the living-room and found the Yellow Pages. There was a box advertisement under the heading 'Night-clubs' which announced that the *Seventh Veil* was a fully licensed venue providing 'intimate entertainment' for a 'select clientèle'. Louise was intrigued. What if she picked up the phone, dialled that number and asked for Gina? Before she knew it she was doing that very thing.

A suave but suspicious-sounding male voice answered. When she asked for Gina he wanted to know who was calling.

'Her sister.'

'Her *what*?' the man said in disbelief. Louise felt affronted. Okay, so they hadn't had much to do with each other over the last few years, but it was painful to realise that Gina never mentioned her. 'Excuse me, I didn't know she had one,' he added semi-apologetically. Even so there was an unpleasant undertone to the man's voice that disturbed her. He was as good as accusing her of lying.

'Please tell her that Louise is on the line,' she said coldly. 'If she's not busy, that is.'

'Gina's always busy. But if you really are her sister I'm sure she can spare you a few minutes. Hold the line, please.'

It was a long wait, but eventually Gina's throaty voice could be heard saying, 'Louise, is it really you? Fancy hearing from my kid sister after all this time. And after midnight, too!'

'I'm sorry if I'm ringing late. . .'

Peals of laughter came. 'Late? My goodness, darling, we never close before three a.m.! But I suppose this is well past your bedtime, isn't it? Still working for that dreary company and married to that dreadful man?'

Louise felt her hackles rise, but she controlled herself and took a deep breath. 'Yes, by the skin of my teeth. Look, I know this is an awful cheek, Gina, but I've simply no one else to turn to. I need somewhere to stay. Just for a week or two, while I sort myself out.' She hesitated before adding, 'You're right about Martin, he's a real loser. And our house is about to be repossessed.'

'You poor thing!' Much to Louise's surprise her sister sounded genuinely sympathetic. 'Of course you can stay at the flat. We've a spare room. Look, why don't you go there now? I'll be back in a couple of hours.'

The idea of a moonlight flit was suddenly extremely attractive. Louise was fully alert, her senses awakening at the prospect of an adventure. 'Could I really? But how would I get in?'

'No problem. You'll find the spare key in the garden, hidden in a statue of Venus by the pool. You know my address, don't you?'

'Are you still in Holland Park, where I sent the Christmas card?'

'That's right. You pop along there right now, and I'll see you as soon as I get back. Help yourself to coffee, booze or whatever you fancy. Oh, there's Ahmed looking daggers at me. Sorry, I have to go. I'm supposed to be with a client. See you soon, though.'

Louise crept into the bedroom where Martin was still snoring loudly, dead to the world. She grabbed a bundle of underwear from a drawer, swept an armful of her clothes and some shoes out of the wardrobe, then went into the bathroom where she hastily freshened up. She dressed herself in a shirt and jeans then retrieved her travel bag from on top of the hall cupboard and packed her things.

Her conscience pricked her as she was about to leave and she wrote a brief note for Martin, telling him she would be in touch. Then, after checking that she had enough cash, she phoned for a taxi and sat hugging her bag just inside the front door, waiting for it to arrive.

The journey across London was swiftly accomplished at that time of night. Gina lived near the park in a large old house that had been converted into flats. Louise entered through wrought iron gates and found herself in a gravelled area containing a central pond, tubs filled with plants and a few rather pretentious-looking statues. She peered at them in the faint light from a towering street-lamp. There was a laughing faun, a rearing unicorn and . . . yes, a small statue that must be Venus, standing in mock-modesty on a shell.

Louise approached and looked beneath it, but there was no sign of a door-key. She reached out and touched the cold stone, convinced that Gina must have meant some other statue. But there were no others remotely resembling the Goddess of Love. Letting her fingers rove over the fluted interior of the shell, Louise grew impatient. Was this some trick?

Then she recalled her sister's exact words: Gina had said 'hidden *in* a statue'. Smiling to herself, Louise let her fingers trail down between the tiny buttocks and then felt between the hard, smooth thighs. A tickling thread brushed her knuckles. She took it between her thumb and forefinger and gave a tug. Out came the key, tinkling against the stone. It had been hidden right inside the anatomically correct figurine.

Giggling softly, Louise crossed the forecourt and used the key in the slot marked Flat 4 to let herself in. She found herself in an elegant hallway, with a marble-topped gilt table and lush pink carpeting that stretched on up the wide stairs. Gina lived on the second floor.

When she entered the apartment and switched on the light Louise was impressed. The main sitting-room was vast and high-ceilinged, and looked as if it had been furnished by an interior designer, with everything just so. Louise wandered round examining the tastefully selected antiques that blended with the more modern furniture, admiring the quality of the furnishings and the subtle understatement of the colour scheme.

Beneath her admiration, however, she was disturbed to detect an unmistakable streak of envy. Defiantly she poured a large gin and tonic from the art deco-style drinks cabinet in the corner and sank into the comforting embrace of the deep sofa, pulling off her shoes. Old feelings were reawakened as she contemplated the fruits of her half-sister's success. 'Ill-gotten gains, more like,' she muttered to herself, taking a long sip of her drink.

All the information Louise had about Gina's career since leaving home had been in the form of rumours, gossip and very occasional meetings. Her sister wasn't one for keeping in touch by letter or phone, and the only time she'd had direct contact with her relatives was at her father's funeral which she had attended briefly, avoiding the aftermath of tea and sympathy. There was no doubt that she was the black sheep of the family, but exactly why this was Louise had never been able to discover.

What she did know was that her sister was far more daring and extrovert than Louise could ever be. She got that from her half-Latin father, of course. When Gina was sixteen and Louise was ten she remembered dark hints being dropped about 'boys'. The elder girl often stayed out late, resulting in angry scenes between Gina and her stepfather Peter, who was their mother's second husband, and Louise's own father. Soon afterwards the precocious fledgling had left the nest, and life at home became very dull. Whatever else Gina had done she'd certainly provided welcome entertainment for a bored ten-year-old girl.

Later, when Louise had reached puberty herself, she missed having her sister around all the more. Sensing that she would have been able to answer her own questions about 'boys', she resented more than ever the fact that Gina had walked out on them. She was also curious about the woman that her sister had become. Still, maybe she could make up for some of that lost time now.

Rising from the depths of the sofa, Louise refilled her glass then wandered off on a tour of the flat. There was a well-equipped kitchen, large enough to take breakfast in, and a luxurious bathroom with a whirlpool bath. There were two doors to the bathroom, the one she'd come in by and another one on the other side that she presumed must lead to a bedroom. Filled with curiosity, she went over and opened it.

It was obvious at once that this was the master bedroom. Decorated entirely in softest pink, with subtle lighting, its air was full of the heady scent of jasmine. Louise was startled to see that the ceiling was covered in mirrored tiles. A king-sized bed dominated the room, and she was somewhat surprised when she noticed a pair of handcuffs hanging from the headrail. She walked over and stroked the exquisite silk cover, relishing the way her bare feet sank into the thick-pile carpet that felt like swansdown between her toes.

Louise was starting to feel deliciously naughty. Like when she had crept into her mother's bedroom as a child and tried on her clothes and make-up. She crossed to the velvet curtains hanging from a brass rail and drew them across, exposing Gina's clothes. And what clothes! There were very few examples of what you might call everyday wear, and only a handful of conventional evening dresses.

The bulk of the collection was made up of exotic and erotic garments in satin, velvet, leather, vinyl and latex. Fascinated, Louise drew out a red latex number with a lace-up back and a see-through panel of black net set into the bosom. She tossed it onto the bed then found an equally outrageous mini-dress in shiny turquoise satin with diagonal slashes of black lace across the breast and crotch.

Her fingers lingered amongst the sensual materials, caressing and scrunching them to feel their sleekness, so eerily like her own skin. Some Louise held up to her cheek, others she draped over herself, trying to imagine how she would look in them. There were accessories too. At the bottom of the wardrobe she could see shiny patent shoes with impossibly high heels, and coiled on hooks were studded leather belts and strange-looking harnesses made of leather, rubber and chains.

'What a weird sex life my sister must have,' she thought, feeling a voyeuristic glee at the thought of her and her partner making love in that very bedroom. She wondered which one of them wore the handcuffs. All she knew about Gina's current partner was that he was called Ahmed. The photo in the paper had been too blurred to make out his features properly. Louise's curiosity grew as she remembered the words on their club ad: 'intimate entertainment'. Gina certainly seemed to be an expert at that if the evidence in her bedroom could be believed.

'I wonder where she keeps her underwear,' Louise thought, and a thrill went through her.

It didn't take her long to find it. There was a row of drawers inside another wardrobe and as she drew them out Louise found sets of bras, panties and suspender belts neatly arranged inside. She pulled out a couple of bras in black lace then realised with a shock that the scanty cups were designed to go *under* the nipples, not over them. The thought proved irresistible. Quickly Louise took off all her clothes and tried on the black bra. Her shapely breasts were thrust upwards, the nipples hardening as they jutted over the supportive padding. She postured in the huge mirror that almost filled one wall, feeling like a calendar girl.

Soon she found some matching undergarments: a skimpy pair of open-crotch panties and a rubber suspender belt. A little more rummaging produced some shiny black plastic stockings which she proceeded to roll up her calves and thighs. The sensation was amazing, like having her legs wrapped in cling film.

Louise finished her second gin then went back to the wardrobe where she selected a pair of black shoes that were about her size. She squeezed her feet into them and sashayed back to the mirror, where she posed seductively, giggling all the while. She hadn't enjoyed herself so much in ages! If only Martin could see me now, she thought. But he was so strait-laced he wouldn't begin to understand what a kick she got out of making herself look so sexy. Impatiently she banished all thoughts of her husband from her mind.

Her eye was drawn back to the two dresses on the bed and she decided to try on the red latex one. The combination of alcohol and fatigue was putting her into a reckless mood, added to which she was feeling decidedly randy. There was something wickedly exhilarating about going through her sister's things without her permission. Especially things like these!

It was quite a struggle getting into the figure-hugging dress and almost impossible to lace up the back. Somehow Louise managed by pulling the ends over her shoulder and tugging, then she knotted them loosely. She looked at herself in the mirror and was shocked to see how low-cut the back was, revealing several inches of buttock cleavage. When she stood back and surveyed herself from the front she gasped with amazement at the vision in the mirror.

Every curve of her body was visible beneath the clingy vinyl, but the biggest surprise was to see her breasts beneath the black netting, pushed up into great peachy mounds by the platform bra. Louise had never imagined she could look so blatantly voluptuous – not without the aid of plastic surgery, anyway. She lifted up one side of her shoulder-length brown hair so that her bosom was tilted provocatively, crossed one thigh half over the other and pointed her toe in a classic pin-up pose. Then she turned round and bent foward, surveying herself over her shoulder as she wiggled her bottom.

Sensing that her voyage of discovery was not yet over, Louise noticed that there were several large drawers under the bed. They were obviously intended for bed linen, but she had a feeling that Gina would have found some other purpose for them. . .

The first drawer she pulled open contained a collection of small whips and riding crops. Louise took one and tried it out. She took up a stern attitude in front of the mirror, looking haughtily down her nose at herself. Had this implement actually been used on someone's backside? If so, whose? She tapped it experimentally against her own behind and felt the faint sting even through the taut plasticised material.

Another drawer yielded a clutter of chains and manacles. Presumably they went with the handcuffs. A third produced an assortment of masks and hoods. She took out a kind of black highwayman's mask edged with frilly lace and fixed it round her head. Gazing upward she saw herself in the mirrored ceiling and the effect was startling, as if she were taking part in some weird ritual.

The last drawer Louise opened made her gasp too, but it also brought an excited flush to her cheeks and a very urgent tingle between her legs. She had uncovered a hoard of dildoes and other sex toys whose striking resemblance to male organs and ingenious design left her in no doubt as to their function.

Tentatively she drew out a huge, flesh-coloured vibrator and ran the artificially ribbed contours across her palm. There was a discreetly-placed switch at the end and when she turned it on the thing leapt into buzzing, throbbing life. It squirmed about in her hands like a live thing. Hastily she turned it off and placed it on the bed. Her fingers moved amongst all kinds of other devices: rings with fleshy rubber prongs attached, pairs of ivory-coloured balls joined by a thread, double dildoes. Most of their uses were blatantly obvious but some she could only guess at. What was also obvious was that she was looking at the assorted paraphernalia of a life devoted entirely to sexual pleasure.

Picking up the large dildo again, Louise felt a languid weariness overcome her and she closed the drawer then lay down on the bed. The duvet cushioned her body deliciously, making her stretch and yawn. She took off the too-tight shoes and the clammy stockings, then began absently stroking her naked thighs with the smooth tip of the artificial glans. Almost without realising it she flicked the switch with her thumb and the noise of an angry mosquito filled the room. Now she could feel it vibrating against her inner thigh, sending electric shock-waves throughout her nervous system. She'd never experienced such a strange sensation before.

Louise felt very woozy as she lay there, drunk and tired but also in a state of high arousal. Her earlier session with Martin had failed to satisfy her, leaving her hungry for what she hadn't had in a long time – a fully satisfying orgasm. The cunning little toy in her right hand was all too tempting. It wasn't long before she was allowing it to nose under the hem of the red dress and over the suspenders towards her already fully awakened vulva.

With a great sigh Louise felt the shuddering tip of the dildo reach her yearning clitoris and she gave a moan of satisfaction at the first stirring contact. Below the nub of hard flesh her pussy felt completely liquid. She moved the fake penis around until she reached the spot that gave her most pleasure, then allowing it to have its head. Soon she was desperate to feel the thing inside her, filling her up. The thick shaft slid easily between her labia and deep into her warm, expanded sex.

By pressing the vibrator upwards, Louise found that she could still apply the necessary friction to her clitoris while she moved the dildo around inside her. She kept it there with one hand while she used the other to caress her breasts through the window of black netting, moving across the bulging slope of flesh to her exposed nipples. The slightly abrasive feel of the material was very stimulating.

Louise arched her back and whimpered as her clitoris throbbed in sympathy with her nipples, and she began to move the thick plastic shaft in and out more rapidly. Her efforts became even more frantic as her lust intensified and soon she was totally oblivious of her surroundings, helplessly caught up in her inexorable rise towards orgasm. All the frustrations of the last few months were driving her on, clamouring for the sweet release into oblivion.

The first spasms of her climax made her cry out,

not in triumphant fulfilment but out of a still more desperate longing. It was a paradox that even in the midst of her satisfaction, even with that thick penis substitute plugging her, she still felt achingly hollow inside. Faintly dissatisfied with herself she pulled the vibrator out of her, silenced it with her thumb and threw it to the end of the bed. For several minutes she lay there sprawled and open, letting the air cool her raw and tingling pussy. Then she turned over on her side and, filled with an exhausted relaxation, finally fell into a deep sleep.

Chapter Two

GINA PUT DOWN the phone and went up to Ahmed, smiling wryly. His dark brown eyes narrowed in suspicion. 'Who was that?'

'You'll never guess. My kid sister!'

'You never told me you had a sister.'

'She's my half-sister, to be precise. Same mother, different dad. I think she's in a bit of a state, so I said she could stay with us for a while.'

Ahmed shrugged. 'As long as she doesn't get in the way.'

'I don't think she will. From what I remember of her, Louise wouldn't say boo to a goose.'

He grinned. 'The submissive kind, eh? Well okay, but if she pokes her nose in where she's not wanted, she'll be out on the street, understood?'

Gina nodded, adjusting her bra. It was a shell-pink satin bra with peepholes through which her tawny nipples protruded. Her only other garments were a minuscule pair of matching panties and suspender belt, black fishnet stockings and shiny black high-heeled shoes. Ahmed's dark eyes smouldered briefly at her before he turned and went into the office behind him.

Proceeding down the corridor, Gina went through a door that took her back into the hushed atmosphere of the Seventh Veil. Subdued lighting afforded a degree of anonymity to the clients who sat at round tables, mostly alone but sometimes with a male friend or two and, very occasionally, with a woman. Even in the semi-darkness it was obvious that most of the audience were Arabs, although there were a few Englishmen too.

Near the door where Gina entered was a raised platform that served as a stage. Six girls were already dancing there to a slow, insinuating beat and soon Gina joined them. She exchanged a smile with Janice, who had only been with them a week but was learning the ropes fast. This was the part of the evening where each girl showed off her talents so that the watching men could choose their favourite. For Gina, though, it was a mere formality. Her man had already been chosen for her by Ahmed. He was a wealthy Egyptian on a brief visit to London who had agreed a fee that was far above anything the other girls could command.

Languidly Gina swayed her hips to the music, enjoying the sensual movement of her muscles, feeling herself relax and become the erotic creature of the night who was now her second self. She was aware of the taut swelling of her breasts filling out the satin bra, and of the hard nipples protruding through their wanton apertures, and she knew that every man in the place desired her. When they discovered that she was already booked they would envy that lucky man, and he would be happy to pay over the odds for her. It was a procedure she had been through many times before. If you wanted the girlfriend of the owner to perform exclusively for you then you paid top dollar, and no arguing.

The pace of the music quickened and Gina rolled her pelvis more suggestively, enjoying the discreet massage that the muscular contractions gave to her sex. She had been to belly-dancing classes and could rival the best of the Arabian dancers, but in the club she performed only a modified version. The clients didn't want to see just an imitation of what they could get at home. What they came to Seventh Veil for was blatant eroticism coupled with a personal service, and the club was already getting a reputation for delivering the goods.

Through the dim lighting Gina surveyed the men's faces as she danced, trying to home in on her target. She could see a man in a long striped *djellabah* sitting at a side table, apart from the rest, and she sensed from his aloof bearing and keen attention to her dancing that he was her client. A burst of excitement flared through her loins. Here was a man who was probably a millionaire, feasting his eyes upon her as if she were his prospective bride. He could look all he liked, and for a handsome sum he would get a very close look indeed, but how far it went was up to her, not him.

Already Gina was wondering what she would grant him, but on the whole she decided she was feeling rather tired and, besides, she was curious to know whether Louise had really followed her directions and ended up back at her flat.

No, let that proud bastard salivate over her as much as he liked, tonight she would keep him in suspense – and later Ahmed would turn him down when he made his discreet enquiries. He would just have to learn that not every woman who acted the whore could be bought. Sometimes that gave her the most pleasure of all.

Gina slowly danced her way towards the man's table, her body glistening with a film of sweat and exuding a mixed aroma of perfume, perspiration and musk. She saw his pupils dilate with interest, and his legs shifted beneath the long white robe. When she was about a metre from his table she paused and stared directly at him, hips still gyrating, her brown eyes giving him just the kind of bold come-on he would find most intriguing.

A waiter cleared the low table next to his chair, leaving only the white cloth on top, and with an agile bound she was soon on top of it. Gina had no worries about falling off, as the table was bolted to the floor and she was well practised in the art of dancing in a restricted space. She watched with a smile as her client's eyes travelled from her shapely ankles up to her long, lean thighs. Out of the corner of her eye she could see that Janice had come to dance for the man at the next table. While she was happy to perform for the man who had paid for her, she didn't like her clients being distracted by neighbouring dancers. But soon the Arab was far too interested in what was, literally, under his nose to bother about what was going on around him.

Concentrating hard to keep her balance, Gina wiggled her body right down until she was squatting before her client and he was looking straight at her bosom. He gave a barely perceptible sigh, which turned into an embarrassed cough. This was his first time at Seventh Veil. She doubted it would be his last. Her hands went to the front fastening of her bra and she snicked it open, letting her breasts hang free beneath the loose pink satin cups with the full extent of her cleavage exposed. She had been blessed with an almost perfect pair, medium-sized and with very long nipples. They were firm and smooth, incredibly inviting to a man's touch, but this man would not get to handle them.

Gina teased him, raising her shoulders to lift the dangling garment and let him peek at the taut slopes of flesh beneath, then letting the bra flop down again. He gave an audible groan and she chuckled, enjoying his discomfiture. Her well-defined pink lips pouted as if she were taking pity on him. She lifted up the satin and let him gaze his fill on the naked delights beneath, then she half-covered herself again and slowly, with great control, swivelled her way back up to a standing position. Her hands smoothed down her hips, drawing attention to the pink triangle that concealed her mons, framed by the long black suspenders. She saw him run the very tip of his tongue between his lips and a tremor of lust took her by surprise.

Balancing carefully on one leg she held up her foot for him, smiling and nodding to indicate that he might remove her shoe. First the Egyptian pressed his lips to the shiny black toe, then he eased it off her heel and placed the shoe in his lap. He repeated the procedure with the other one then placed the pair carefully on the carpet beside his chair. His hands returned to his lap, where Gina was sure she could detect slight movement beneath the flowing robe. Was the man wearing any underwear at all? Somehow she doubted it.

Standing on tiptoe, Gina twirled around to the music and showed him her buttocks, leaning forward and thrusting them almost in his face. She began to caress them, letting her fingers slip right under the leg of her panties and stroke the deep chasm between her cheeks. This seemed to get him extremely aroused. She could hear his breath coming in sharp, ragged bursts as he ravished her with his eyes. So he was a bum man, was he? Well, she had a treat in store for him!

Turning again, Gina decided to free herself from the bra. She removed it and let it hang from her fingers, dangling against the tip of the man's nose. He sniffed it appreciatively and she let it fall into his lap. Eagerly he caught it up and pressed it to his face, eyes closed, breathing in the lingering vapours. Then he looked up and saw her hands lifting her bare breasts for his inspection, the pinkish-brown nipples already jutting and stiff. He moaned, and his hands dropped to his lap again, still clutching the skimpy garment like a totem.

Slowly she unhooked the suspenders from her stockings and began to roll them down, with his dark eyes watching every inch of her flesh as it was uncovered. Peeling the last few inches off her toes she dangled the stocking before him then let it fall into his lap. Again he gathered it up in both hands and pressed it to his face, inhaling deeply. She repeated the process with the other stocking and then undid her suspender belt and let it fall to the table. Now only a scant few inches of pink satin covered the last vestige of her modesty.

It was time to slow the pace. Gina always liked this part, where she had them really lusting after her but she denied them that last glimpse. It made her feel both sexy and powerful. She smiled to see him gazing up at her like a supplicant, his eyes roving all over her body, the hands in his lap moving restlessly over what she was now sure was a giant erection beneath. She turned slowly, bending forward a little so that her pert buttocks were displayed to advantage, and heard him groan again. Definitely a bum man.

Well, she would give him what he wanted – but slowly. First her hands slipped beneath the top of her satin pants to cup her bum cheeks, clutching and stroking them as she gradually allowed the pink covering to slip down. Gina glanced down over her shoulder at him and saw that he was holding his erection firmly beneath the thin cotton of his robe. His dark eyes were staring at her with glazed intensity. Leaning forward a bit more she parted the two halves of her behind and gave him a peek at the rosy crevice between them, which elicited a sharp gasp of surprised gratification.

Moving her hips in a slinky rhythm, Gina rotated her bum at him and let her panties finally slip down her thighs. She daintily stepped out of them and threw them back over her shoulder into his lap, then she turned round with a winsome smile and presented him with her totally naked body. She watched his face contort for a few seconds, his hands moving furtively, and then he made a series of groaning noises and she knew that, for the time being at least, her client was satisfied.

Leaping nimbly down to the floor Gina gathered up her scattered undies and whipped the white cloth off the table around her naked body like a toga. She gave the Egyptian a brief kiss on his fevered brow as the waiter moved in to settle the account. Then she flitted off through the other tables, like a ghost in the white sheet, until she could slip through the exit and into the dressing-room at the back of the stage.

Ahmed was waiting for her there. 'How did it go?' he asked. 'Was he satisfied?'

Gina unwound the tablecloth and sprayed her face and bosom with delicately scented toilet water as a quick freshener. Soon the room was full of the aroma of lilac. 'I should say so!' she grinned.

He came up and kissed her cheek. 'Good, then he'll be back.' His hand crept up to the lower slope of her breast which he stroked delicately.

Gina removed his hand with gentle firmness and went to put on a pair of white cotton pants. She didn't bother with a bra but slipped into the loose comfort of grey cotton track-pants and hooded top. 'I want to go home now,' she announced. 'Will you come too, or do you have to stay on a while?'

'No, I'll be back after I've had a word with chummy-boy. See you in five minutes.'

He kissed her briefly on the mouth but it was enough to rouse her libido. She usually felt randy after she'd been performing all night, and Ahmed reaped the benefit. Tonight, though, there was another dimension to her excitement. She was keen to get back and see if her kid sister was there.

Gina's curiosity about how she looked these days was growing by the minute. The last time she'd seen her was at her wedding, when Louise had been the traditional blushing bride. What a farce! She'd almost turned down the invitation but then had taken pity on her sister at the last minute. Well, it seemed her prediction that Martin would turn out to be as big an idiot as he looked had come true.

They got back to their Kensington flat at two in the morning. Gina knew at once that Louise had arrived because she'd left the light on in the living-room. A quick inspection also revealed that she'd helped herself to a gin and tonic, leaving both bottles out on the cabinet.

'Maybe she's in the spare room,' Gina said, giving Ahmed a wink.

He followed her as she went to find out, but before she reached the spare room Gina noticed that a faint glow was coming from her own bedroom. She pushed the door open. The room looked a mess, with her wardrobe curtains flung open and the drawers pulled out from under the bed. But it was what was on top of the bed that made her gasp aloud.

Louise was lying there wearing her own red latex dress, which was hitched up around her waist to reveal black suspenders and open-crotched panties through which the pale pink lips of her pussy could be clearly seen. She glanced at Ahmed, whose eyes were nearly popping out of his head. 'The little minx!' she whispered. Then she noticed that lying beside her sister on the bed was her favourite vibrator. The glistening film over its plastic glans left her in no doubt that it had provided good service.

'What a cheek!' she giggled, tiptoeing over to the bed.

Ahmed murmured, 'If you ask me she's just asking for a severe spanking.'

Gina turned, her finger against her mouth. 'Well, well, well! Who'd have thought it? My naughty little sister!'

After pulling the duvet up over her sister's sleeping form, Gina led Ahmed back towards the door. 'Let's leave her to sleep it off,' she said once they were out of the room. 'We can use the sofa bed just for tonight.'

'I don't care, as long as I get to have you,' he grinned. 'It's a good thing I didn't come back from the club alone, or I wouldn't have been able to resist her. What a sister!'

'Now don't get the wrong idea,' Gina cautioned him. 'I know she looks pretty raunchy right now, but that's not the Louise I remember. It could be she's just drunk and in a state over the break-up of her marriage. I don't think she's normally so . . . uninhibited.'

When they returned to the living-room Ahmed was so eager to make love that he practically tore the clothes off Gina. They ended up on the floor, with each of them mouthing the other's private parts. Gina groaned her approval of the solid dimension of her lover's penis as it worked its way towards the back of her throat. She relaxed and let the huge glans move in rhythm while Ahmed's tongue played delicately around her engorged clitoris.

It was such a relief, after all the tensions of the evening, to feel herself being coaxed towards orgasm by the man who knew exactly how to make her come. Gina let her tongue move lazily up and down his shaft while Ahmed began the regular pattern of licking and sucking that never failed to induce an orgasm. His hand reached for the nearest breast and tweaked her already rock-hard nipple, notching up her arousal to fever-pitch.

With unconscious grace Gina began rotating her pelvis to bring herself to the brink, at the same time tasting the first bitter juices that seeped from her lover's glans. Maybe they would climax together, she thought dreamily. It was good to do that straight away, before they fucked. Her fingers caressed his balls, feeling them tighten in readiness to expel his seed, and she knew her own orgasm was imminent. When she felt his finger thrust inside her she squeezed hard and the throbbing excitement rose to exquisite, unbearable heights until there was a sudden change and she was swept into the cataclysm, her whole body shuddering as the rippling first orgasm intensified and then, very gradually, diminished.

The first few drops of his ejaculation tickled her throat before he withdrew and spurted over her naked breasts, rubbing the viscous mess all over her nipples the way she liked it and prolonging the last few seconds of her ecstasy. She looked up at him, eyes shining, and murmured, 'It looks like we're both turned on more than usual tonight. I wonder why?'

He laughed and turned her over, starting to massage her plump buttocks and making the whole of her rear end glow with delicious warmth. 'She doesn't look like you,' he said. 'Not from what I saw of her, anyway. Her tits are smaller, and her pussy lips are all pale and virginal-looking.'

'I wouldn't be surprised if her wimp of a husband never satisfied her. Maybe that's why their marriage is on the rocks.' Gina got onto her knees with her rump thrust provocatively in the air and let Ahmed caress her thighs, itching for his fingers to move into the slick chasm between them. He was in no hurry, teasing her labia with the lightest of fingertip brushes before he finally moved in.

'Ah!' she groaned her approval, feeling a hot wave of renewed sensuality pass through her at the first firm caress of his fingers. She looked back over her shoulder and saw that his erection was growing again. He deftly unrolled a thickly ribbed condom down its length. She shuddered in anticipation and she began to rotate her buttocks in automatic response.

There was one last fondle of her buttocks and then Gina felt the hard nose of his prick easing between her labia. She gave a long sigh as he penetrated her deeply, filling her up and making her arch her back and throw back her head in cat-like delight. Ahmed's hands moved to her belly, clutching at her smooth flesh while his mouth nibbled at the nape of her neck, sending her into new paroxysms of bliss.

Gina felt herself rising towards a second climax. Ahmed's right hand moved up to her breast while his left moved down to her mons, where he proceeded to give her clitoris exactly the kind of delicate friction that would speed up her progress. Gina ground her buttocks against his stomach in a fast rhythm, encouraging him to increase the pace of his thrusts so that the rubber profiles on the condom would give a good massage to her vaginal walls. He took the hint and soon they were both thrusting hard in pursuit of the ultimate pleasure.

This time, however, Ahmed was so excited that he jumped the gun, coming with spectacular force and triggering Gina as the violent spurts made him gasp out loud. She rode the tidal wave of her orgasm with spectacular abandon, screaming out her rapture as her whole body convulsed in fiery spasms and finally collapsing onto her knees when all the wild energy was spent. They lay together on the carpet for a while, quietly nuzzling each other, until Gina decided to pull out the sofa and get the bedding from its innards so they could get some well-earned rest.

'Tomorrow we'll find out just what Louise has been up to,' she murmured, as she snuggled against Ahmed's warm, hairy chest and waited for sleep to envelop her.

It was Louise who found them in the morning as she stumbled into the living-room with several mischievous demons using her head as a pin cushion.

'Oh sorry!' she gasped, waking Gina at once although Ahmed remained sound asleep.

Gina noticed that Louise was wearing her dressing-gown. She grinned and slipped out of the covers, pulling on her leggings and sweatshirt. Once they were both in the kitchen she closed the door behind them then gave her sister a hug.

'Hi! Good to see you.'

Louise pulled a face. 'I can't look too good this morning. Not after last night. I'm afraid I drank rather too much of your gin.'

'No problem. You sounded pretty fed up on the phone. Want to talk about it?'

'Later, perhaps. Right now I could murder for a cup of coffee.'

While they waited for the coffee to perc Gina gave her sister a quick inspection. Despite her rumpled, hung-over look, Louise had retained her pretty face and good figure. The light brown hair that now hung dishevelled to her shoulders was obviously well cared for, and could easily be restored to glossy stylishness. Her complexion was clear and even, her eyes still that intriguing mix of green and brown, and the generous curve of her upper lip was balanced by a sensual fullness in the lower one.

Gina's gaze dropped to the high, protruding breasts and the slim waist accentuated by the tightly-tied belt. Whatever tribulations her kid sister had undergone she hadn't turned to bingeing, at least. She found herself assessing Louise as a potential dancer for the club and gave a wry smile, turning her attention to the coffee.

With a hot drink inside her Louise visibly relaxed. 'It's really good of you to put me up. I don't know what I'd have done without you. I was at the end of my tether last night.'

'Was Martin being violent towards you?'

'Not exactly. I just can't stand being around him any more. We're horrendously in debt and stand to lose the house, but he's still drinking and gambling. I felt I had to get away.'

Gina knew Ahmed wouldn't tolerate having her around for too long. They needed the flat to themselves, especially when they brought special clients home.

'You're welcome to stay here for a week or so, but it might be best if you started looking for a place of your own.' Then she remembered what Louise had been wearing when she found her last night, sprawled on her bed. She grinned. 'I know you've already been exploring my wardrobe. That was really rather naughty of you.'

Louise clapped her hand to her mouth. 'Oh, my God! I'm awfully sorry. I was half out of my head. I'd never have behaved like that normally.'

'Well, at least you have no illusions about what line of business I'm in. The club that Ahmed and I run entertains businessmen. Mostly foreigners on business trips to London. We hold some specialist nights, so I have an extensive collection of costumes.'

'Not just clothes,' Louise pointed out, the hint of a twinkle in her eye.

'No, we do offer a full range of services. Fortunately I'm in a position to pick and choose my clients. We run an upmarket operation, Lou. Our clients are very wealthy and we're as careful about admitting them as any gentleman's club.'

'You charge a lot, then?'

Gina nodded. 'Oh yes, our girls are very well paid.' She paused, eyeing her sister soberly for a moment. 'Tempted?'

Louise gave a laugh of derision. 'You can't be serious!'

'Oh yes I am. We have several dancers paying off their debts by working for us. And it won't take them that long. Once they're back on their financial feet they can stop doing it, if they want to. Only I've a feeling that most of them will carry on. They get to enjoy it after a while.'

Louise pulled a disbelieving face. '*Like* it? Surely a whore is a whore, whatever level she's operating at.'

Gina poured them both more coffee and lit herself a cigarette. She saw her sister make a slight grimace and remembered that her smoking had caused quite a few rows before she'd left home.

'I don't think you quite understand. Okay, sometimes our girls do sleep with the clients, but not as a matter of course. They're first and foremost erotic dancers. They strip off and perform at the tables. If they want to take it further with a particular gentleman that's entirely up to them, but they don't have to.'

'So they're more like strip-tease artistes?'

'Yes, except that they are all excellent dancers and they strut their stuff right in front of the clients. The men get a close-up view of what's on offer. But they can't touch, not unless the girl gives them explicit permission. We're very strict about that.'

'I see.'

'Maybe you'd like to come along one night and see for yourself?'

She saw Louise shrink back into her seat. 'Oh no, I don't think so.'

Gina shrugged. 'It's up to you. Do you have a job at the moment?'

'Yes, but maybe not for much longer. They're

planning to lay off some staff.'

'Well then.'

The women were interrupted by the sudden appearance of Ahmed, who came in wearing a towelling robe and yawning. He gave Louise a nod and made for the coffee pot.

'Say hello nicely, Ahmed!' Gina said sternly.

'It's okay, I expect he's tired.' Louise broke in. 'I'm sorry I stole your bed, Ahmed. It won't happen again.'

'You bet!' Ahmed grunted. 'What shall we do with her, Gina? Smack her bottom, that's my suggestion.'

Gina pretended to be affronted. 'I want none of that talk in front of my little sister. She's not one of the showgirls, Ahmed. She's led a sheltered life, haven't you, Lou?'

'I suppose so. By your standards, at least.'

Ahmed swallowed most of his coffee in one gulp then said, 'Well she'll get her eyes opened while she's here, won't she?'

Gina said nothing, but privately resolved to keep the pair of them apart as far as possible. Not that she was jealous, it was more that she wished to protect her sister. Despite the gulf between them she was family, after all, and as she grew older that was starting to mean something.

'Well, if you don't mind I'm going back to bed,' Ahmed announced. 'I like a lie-in on a Sunday morning. Coming, Gina?'

Louise said, 'Go ahead, I'll be okay. I think I'll take a walk, maybe buy a newspaper. Shall I take a spare key?'

Once Louise had left, Ahmed fell on Gina and dragged her back to the bedroom. He pulled down her leggings and was soon inside her, pumping away deliciously. Gina groaned and wriggled her way towards a climax, but as the familiar feelings accelerated inside her she couldn't help wondering whether the presence of another woman in the flat had turned her lover on. He wasn't usually this randy after a late night.

Still, who was she to complain?

Chapter Three

IT WAS STRANGE going to work from Gina's flat for the first time. Inconvenient, too. Louise had to take the Underground halfway across London and then walk, which meant getting up an hour earlier than usual. Obviously she couldn't carry on like that for long.

When she looked for flats in the evening paper, however, she was horrified by what she would have to pay out in rent. There was no way she could afford that on her salary, especially as she hoped to shoulder her share of the mortgage debt as well. She phoned Martin from work and left a brief message on the answerphone telling him that she was okay and would be coming back to the house to fetch her things at some point.

Meanwhile, Louise tried to keep out of her sister's way as much as possible. She didn't get back to the flat until around seven, by which time Gina and Ahmed were preparing to go to the *Seventh Veil*. On Monday night she was invited along, but she declined, saying she wanted an early night. Even so, she couldn't help feeling curious about what went on at their club.

After a ready-made supper, courtesy of Marks and Spencer, Louise thought she would watch some television and looked around for the remote control. She eventually found it in a cupboard (evidently they weren't great TV watchers) but on the same shelf were some photograph albums. Curious to see if they held any family photos, she took the pile out and sat down on the carpet to look through them.

The first one she opened had some pictures of Gina's father in the front. She had inherited his dark, Latin looks and probably his fiery temperament too if their mother could be believed. Flicking on through the pages Louise came across some photos she recognised. There were some shots taken of the pair of them in the back garden of the Pimlico house, Louise smiling brightly and Gina scowling. It had evidently been taken in the summer because they were both in bikinis, Louise still flat-chested and little-girlish at nine, while Gina had already blossomed into a buxom teenager with a slim waist and long, lean legs. No wonder all the boys had been after her, Louise thought.

There were photos from a seaside holiday in Devon too, the last time she remembered them all being together, her mother and father and the two girls. It made her sad to think how the whole family had broken up soon after, with first Gina and then her own father leaving home until only she and her mother were left. Two years later, their mother had died of cancer. Louise thought that was why she'd sought out Gina once her marriage failed – she had no one closer to turn to.

Putting aside the family album Louise picked up a second one. A tingle of excitement went through her when she realised that these pictures had been taken at the club. The first few showed girls dancing on a stage in various states of undress, and Gina was amongst them. From their positions it was clear that they were making some very sexy moves, and in the dimness beyond several pairs of eyes could be seen gleaming with intense concentration.

Louise turned the page and saw photos of individual girls dancing on the table tops for appreciative males. She was amazed to see how close they got to their clients, thrusting their naked breasts right into the men's faces. Although she was embarrassed by the blatant exhibitionism she was also fascinated. How did it feel to have that much power over a man, to prance before him on a 'look but don't touch' basis and make him salivate at the sight of your naked body? She couldn't possibly bring herself to do it, of course, but she was still intrigued by the idea. Maybe Gina would tell her about it in detail sometime.

But there were some still more intriguing photographs to come. In another album she could see Gina in what looked like fancy dress at some kind of party where everyone wore outlandishly sexy clothes. Her sister wore a kind of black rubber corset with holes cut in it for her breasts, a tiny pair of spangly silver panties and thigh-high shiny boots with spiky heels. Her hair was fluffed up to form an enormous halo around her head and she had great panda eyes and red lips.

When she turned the pages of the same album

Louise found many more peculiar photos: Gina dressed as a nurse, Gina dressed as a school-marm, caning an overgrown schoolboy's behind; Gina dressed in an elegant ball gown and wielding a serious-looking dildo. The variations filled several pages and left Louise totally flabbergasted. This was another world, and one she wasn't sure she wanted to explore in real life. Yet to see it recorded by the camera was a fascinating experience.

Louise replaced the albums in the cupboard and turned on the television but her mind was still on those extraordinary photographs. Then she noticed a pile of videos on a shelf and her heartbeat quickened. Chances were she knew exactly what kind of videos they would be. She got to her feet and went over to read the labels on their spines.

They were labelled after the days of the week and Louise guessed they had been taken at the club. Gina had said they held special theme parties so they must be films of the proceedings. With trembling fingers Louise took down one subtitled 'SV – Fetish Night'.

The video opened with a crowd of people laughing and joking, playing to the camera. Louise spotted Gina at once. She had on an extraordinary pair of shoes, so high-heeled they must have been extremely uncomfortable to walk in, and what looked like a couple of plastic bags fashioned into a bikini. The camera followed her on to the stage, where there were other girls dressed in high-heeled shoes, all very shiny and bright. Gina sat down on the kind of low stool you get in shoe shops and a red-haired woman came up and knelt before her, almost as if she were worshipping her feet. She removed one of the shoes reverently and began to kiss Gina's toes.

The video grew even more bizarre. The red-haired woman took Gina's shoe and began to masturbate with its pointed toe. Louise found that bit so weird that she fast-forwarded until she came to a new scene. Men were being invited up on stage to have their penises fondled by women wearing rubber gloves. Again, this was more than Louise could take. She removed the video from the slot in the machine and gingerly picked out another one.

This one, subtitled 'Bed Time', was totally different. It was an intimate film of Gina and Ahmed making love in the same bed in which Louise had slept when she arrived. At first she felt guilty watching it, like a voyeuse, but then she told herself that they were used to doing it in front of other people, so why worry?

As she watched her sister performing fellatio on her lover, and then lowering herself with great enthusiasm onto the hard spike of his erection, Louise felt something akin to envy. Gina was so uninhibited, so obviously enjoying herself in a sensual and voluptuous fashion. Had it ever been like that between her and Martin? Not that she could remember, and certainly not in the last couple of years.

Now, watching Gina use her pelvis with supple grace, groaning with delight as Ahmed's fingers crept up to caress her huge nipples, Louise admitted to herself that she'd been missing out. Their love-making was going on and on, a far cry from the five or so minutes of frenzied activity that she had known with Martin. Often she had been left unsatisfied afterwards but he had ignored her needs and selfishly gone straight to sleep. Even bringing herself off with the vibrator had been a more thrilling experience than most of her times with her husband.

Self-pity threatened to overwhelm her so she stopped the video and put it back in the cupboard. Then she decided to have a bath. She made full use of the expensive toiletries she found, luxuriating in the scented water and satin-smooth body cream. The erotic sights she had seen that evening had made her yearn with unsatiated desire, but she had no idea how long she would have to wait to find a new partner. Then she remembered her sister's impressive collection of sex aids. Did she dare make use of them again?

Louise glanced at the clock: half past eleven. She knew it would be hours before the pair of them came home from the club, so she went into their room and pulled out the drawer from under the bed. This time she examined the contents more closely. Amongst the various sizes and shapes of dildo she found a pot of cream called 'Afrodisiana'. Squinting at the small print she saw that it was supposed to contain extracts of rare African plants that worked as aphrodisiacs. It was recommended for use in conjunction with a dildo. She unscrewed the lid and put it to her nose. It smelled kind of mossy and herbal and half of it had already been used.

She chose a thick wand of ivory plastic as her penis substitute, lay down on the thick-pile carpet (somehow Gina's bed seemed taboo after seeing that video) and opened up her robe. After the relaxing bath her skin felt warm and smooth, inviting to the touch of her own fingers. She'd borrowed a pillow for her head and felt perfectly comfortable, a deep-down feeling of anticipation making her glow all over. Tonight she would discover what it meant to be a truly sensual woman.

Louise put her finger into the pot and spread the cool cream over her labia. It felt icy cold at first but then it began to burn a little, like cool fire. She felt the delicate tissues start to tingle and throb until her clitoris became ultra-sensitive, bulging out from between her labia. She stroked it gently and the most wonderful sensations flooded through her, making her squirm and moan in delight.

Forgetting all about the dildo that lay at her side, she continued to stroke herself with light, fluttering movements of her fingertips. The deep need for fulfilment soon made her rub more firmly as the slippery nub swelled up, demanding more of her. It was just like scratching an irritating itch, only a hundred times more satisfying. She could feel herself becoming more and more wet, flooding her inner labia with sticky juices and making it easier for her fingers to slide back and forth over her clitoris that was becoming ever more hungry for stimulation. Like a ravenous animal it reared and stiffened at her touch, frightening her with the violence of her own need.

Yet however long she persevered her climax seemed just as far away. She was stuck on a high plane of arousal, but no amount of friction seemed to take her higher to that final, blissful release. Her wrist ached and she wondered how much longer she could keep going. Then she remembered that the cream was supposed to be used in conjunction with a dildo, and she reached for the hard implement at her side. Over and over again she plunged it into her heated vagina, clenching her muscles to draw it in and then pushing out to expel it again. Her body was beyond her control, acting out of some fevered instinct that was pushing her towards a conclusion she both craved and dreaded.

At long last the sensations suddenly intensified, propelling her into a self-obliterating orgasm that set the lower half of her body convulsing with almost painful contractions. Louise gasped and moaned her way through the experience and then lay limp and exhausted, her heart pounding rapidly in her chest and her limbs trembling. She had no idea how long she had been lying there by the time Gina returned.

'Oh, you wicked girl! When the cat's away the mouse will play, is that it?' she said with mock reproof when she walked in through the bedroom door.

Louise opened her eyes and tried to sit up, but she flopped back down onto the floor again, utterly spent. Gina frowned as she picked up the pot of cream. 'You haven't been using this on yourself, have you?' Louise nodded. 'You silly thing! You should have asked me about it.'

'Why?' Louise asked, faintly.

'It's for internal use only. You put it on the end of the dildo and it gives you a stronger climax. But if you use it too soon, or put it on your clitoris, the effect can be quite painful.'

'You can say that again!'

'You poor thing! Still, that'll teach you to play with fire, won't it?'

'I'm sorry, Gina. I've got no excuse this time. I wasn't drunk or anything, I just. . .' To her dismay Louise felt the tears start to roll. Comforting arms supported her and thrust a tissue under her nose. She was aware of Gina's musky perfume and felt a faint aftershock of arousal.

'I know what you need,' her sister said. 'A hot chocolate laced with brandy. Then we can talk, if you want.'

While Gina went into the kitchen to prepare the drinks, Louise cried into the tissue. She felt such a fool, apart from anything else.

Wrapped in the warm robe, Louise went through to the living-room and sank into the huge sofa where Gina soon joined her. As she sipped the rich, sweet drink she began to relax again.

'It's all right, you know. I don't mind,' her sister said, grinning over the top of her mug.

Louise smiled back. 'You weren't supposed to find out. I thought I'd be safely tucked up in bed by the time you returned from the club.'

'I knocked off early. Thought you might want to chat. You're in a bit of a state really, aren't you, Lou?'

She nodded. 'I'm starting to realise what a total shit Martin is. And I've been putting up with it for so long. I should have left him years ago.'

'I did warn you. At your wedding, if I

remember rightly. Still, I'm not going to say "I told you so" because there's no point. The question is, where do you go from here?'

'I've no idea. When I think of all the money I owe it's frightening. I can't go on managing alone on my salary, and what if I lose my job?'

'You know, I think you really should consider joining us at the club. It's not as bad as you might think. Of course, you have to dance with some conviction, act really sexy. But half the time it's just that, an act. You may be going through the motions but your mind can be somewhere else.'

Louise drained her mug, savouring the pool of liquid chocolate at the bottom. Should she tell Gina about seeing the photos, the videos? She decided against it. Her copybook was already blotted enough for one night. 'I'm not like you, Gina. I've had no experience of that sort of thing. You've always been more adventurous than me.'

Gina gave a naughty smile, her brown eyes gleaming. 'But it seems to me that you have a healthy curiosity about sex, Louise. Why else would you go snooping around my bedroom?'

'I'm curious, yes. But I'm also a bit afraid.'

'What of? Maybe you fear that you'll become insatiable, throwing yourself at every man who comes your way.'

Louise made a wry face. 'I don't think there's much chance of that. I'll be lucky if Martin hasn't put me off the male sex for life.'

'Is that why you're going in for so much DIY these days?'

Following a spontaneous urge, Louise threw a cushion at her sister. Gina caught it with a laugh and threw it back. Her fingers played with a strand of dark hair as she tucked her bare feet under her in the big armchair. 'You know, you really should come along one night,' she continued. 'Just to see things for yourself.'

'I might.'

Gina picked up a cigarette pack from the dresser and took one out. 'How about tomorrow? It's a normal night – normal for us, anyway. Nothing too outlandish going on. And Ahmed will take care of you, see that you're not harassed or anything.'

Louise glanced at the clock. 'Well, if I'm going to take up your offer I'd better make sure I get to bed now. Otherwise I won't be able to keep my eyes open.'

She rose and went over to give Gina a kiss on the cheek. 'Thanks for everything. I don't know what I would have done without you.'

Lying in the spare bed, Louise reflected on the differences between them. Just how much experience had her sister packed in during the past twelve years? She really did feel like the naive younger sibling, even though they were both adults now. And yes, she was curious about Seventh Veil and what went on there. Maybe she should overcome her scruples and take up Gina's invitation to attend.

After all, she was starting a new life now, one without Martin. A wave of misery threatened to swamp her as she thought of their failed marriage, but there was something exciting about it too. They had married too young, everyone had said so, but the bonus was that she was still young enough to enjoy life and find someone new.

*

At work the next day a cloud of gloom hung over the offices of Newbolt & Co. Rumours abounded of imminent redundancies and Louise knew she could be in the firing line – literally! Everyone was watching the personnel manager like a hawk, trying to read his inscrutable expression, but nothing happened. Even so, when the end of the day came there were no sighs of relief, only groans at the thought that the suspense would continue.

Travelling back to Holland Park in a crowded tube train Louise reflected that she could really do with something to take her mind off work that evening. Provided she had time for a rest she would go with Gina to the club and check it out for herself. The flat was empty when she arrived, so she took a quick shower and left a note on the kitchen table saying she was taking a nap but would like to accompany them to Seventh Veil later.

When Louise awoke from her slumbers she could hear Gina singing to herself in the kitchen. She got up and went in to find her cooking pasta.

'Thought you might like something before we go,' her sister smiled. 'It'll be a long night. But I'm really glad you've decided to come. You'll enjoy it, I can guarantee!'

Ahmed was already there, it seemed, and Gina had to perform that evening but she promised that Louise would be well looked after. When she expressed doubts about her limited wardrobe Gina offered to let her wear any of her clothes.

'Nothing too conspicuous though, I suggest. Not unless you want to stand out in the crowd, that is.'

After much deliberation, Louise decided on a slinky velvet dress in hyacinth blue. It was smart and sexy enough for evening wear without being too obvious. She let Gina do her hair in a new, swept-back style that accentuated the heart shape of her face. It was a nice feeling to have her big sister brush her hair again, reminding her of the days when they still lived together.

'Come on, we're going to be late and Ahmed will be mad at me,' Gina announced at last. 'He hates it when I keep a client waiting.'

They took a taxi all the way to Park Lane where the club was situated in a basement. 'Near to all the posh hotels,' as Gina explained. The doorman smiled and inclined his head as they walked in. Louise's eyes took a while to adjust to the dim light and somewhere in the heart of the complex she could hear the thumping beat of some raunchy music. Gina moved through the corridors and offices greeting everyone until Ahmed appeared.

'Where the hell have you been?' he said.

'Ssh, don't be a spoilsport. We're here now. What's on my agenda tonight?'

'Ravi wants a personal, Hamid wants a feelie and Chuck wants a special.'

'Well he can't have one. Tell him next time. He can have a feelie tonight.'

'Okay. Oh, there's a new guy called Shamooz. Top brass at Technoleum. Be nice to him.'

'Right. Where's he sitting?'

'Table seven. Lucky for some! Now you go and get ready. The girls are well into their routine. Take the solo spot. Don't worry about your sister, I'll take care of her.'

Louise listened to their exchange in wide-eyed amazement, wondering what it all meant. When Gina disappeared into the dressing-room Ahmed took her by the elbow and steered her through a door on the left and into a large dark room in which only red lamps burned except at the bar and on stage. The ruby glow cast over everything took some getting used to, but when Louise sat down with Ahmed at an empty table and looked towards the more brightly lit stage her eyes soon became accustomed to the weird half-light.

Ahmed clicked his fingers at a waiter who came up at once. 'Champagne!' came the order. Louise didn't want to argue. Instead she looked with increasing wonder at the girls who were gyrating semi-nude on the small platform. Their erotic dances and minimal costumes were obviously designed to show off their very attractive bodies. Then she noticed some business going on between a client and one of the waiters. It wasn't long before a girl was wending her way from the stage to his table, and Louise realised that the clientèle could order more than just drinks.

'We like to have our waiters acting as go-betweens,' Ahmed explained. His tone was oddly formal, like that of a tourist guide. 'That way no one is offended and the business is conducted with propriety. A system of discreet hand signals is used.'

'I see. And what range of services is on offer, exactly?'

'The basic consists of a table dance only, with no touching. A lap dance allows the girl to slide into the man's lap and wriggle about. No touching is permitted. Both these dances take place in public. There is a private area where a client may have a ''feelie'', which allows touching above the girl's waist only. Naturally, that is the most expensive of all.'

'And afterwards?'

Ahmed's black eyes met hers sternly. 'That is entirely between the girl and the client.'

The cold way he talked about the 'girls' was rather chilling, but Louise supposed he had to keep a rational business head. However it suggested that if she should decide to join his staff she could expect no special privileges for being Gina's relative.

'Watch Janice!' Ahmed commanded, nodding in the girl's direction. 'You will see what a basic dance entails. Generally it lasts about five minutes.'

'Is that all?'

'It is quite long enough to satisfy most of our clients. The preliminary dancing on stage acts as a kind of appetiser, you see. By the time an individual girl arrives at their table the men are already well aroused.'

The table dance began with the girl asking the man to help her up. She put one high-heeled shoe into his palm for a few seconds then stepped nimbly onto the table where she proceeded to undulate her body. She quickly removed the top half of her bikini so that her small breasts were on view. For a while she danced topless, caressing her nipples and rousing them to hard pink points. Then she let her hands slip down to her stomach and made faces at the man while she slipped her fingers into her panties and appeared to play with herself.

Louise looked around her, peering into the shadows where most of the audience sat with their eyes intently focused on the stage. Only a few were distracted by the sight of the table dancer who was now inching down her pants to display her sand-coloured pussy. The man she was dancing for leaned forward in his chair to inspect her more closely. She wiggled a few more times, dangling her discarded garments in front of the man's nose, then skipped down from the table and wrapped her naked body in the table-cloth, teasing her client with her eyes as she did so. There was a glimpse of her bare rump as she dashed off towards the stage door, weaving between the tables.

Turning her attention back to the stage Louise noticed that Gina had appeared, resplendent in a kind of jewelled bikini and shiny silver stockings, held up by white furry suspenders. Looking back at Ahmed she noticed his eyes widen, and his lips curved into a kind of proprietary smile.

'She looks great, doesn't she?' Louise said.

He nodded, but at once rose from his chair. 'Excuse me for a moment.'

She saw him go over to a man sitting in the corner and hold a brief conversation. Her gaze returned to the stage where it was already evident that Gina was a star amongst the dancers. Where they merely wiggled, she gyrated; where they acted slinky, she was voluptuous; where they were vulgarly sexy she was exquisitely erotic. Gina was a class act, and no mistake.

'I wonder how much *she* makes a night,' Louise thought, and was instantly ashamed of herself. It was none of her business.

Slowly, seductively, Gina came to the front of the little stage and began to descend the steps. All the men's eyes were on her as she made her slow, sinuous progress across the room, moving her body with proud grace. It was obvious that everyone was envying the man who would have her special favour that night. The man in question sat smugly awaiting her with Ahmed at his side, and soon she was standing in front of him. A waiter came with a light bamboo screen and placed it around the table, but he left an opening through which Louise could see what was going on.

Ahmed picked up the champagne bottle, poured the man another glass and handed it to him, then helped Gina onto the low table. Louise had the feeling that some pre-arranged programme was being acted out as the dance began. She could just see her sister's dark eyes flashing in the glare from the stage but her body had turned a rosy pink all over from the dim reddish lighting.

Some of the other girls were moving from the stage to various tables around the room, but Louise found it impossible to look anywhere else. She was fascinated by the sight of her sister's lithe body as it twisted and turned on the high heels, her hips swaying extravagantly while her stomach moved in rippling circles. Her hands were under her breasts, lifting them up for the man's inspection, and then she began slowly working the thin straps down her arms, accentuating the deep ravine that divided her bosom.

Ahmed resumed his seat at Louise's side. 'That

man's bought himself a feelie,' he announced matter-of-factly, shifting his chair to get a better view. 'But I doubt he'll be using his hands very much. Watch.'

Gina wriggled out of her bra straps so that the cups were held up by sheer will power. She knelt down and the man moved closer so that his nose was almost in her cleavage. With agonising slowness she turned down the top of one bra cup. Lower and lower it went until the brownish areola of her nipple was exposed. Then she did the same with the other one. The bra hung there provocatively, almost revealing all but not quite, while the man stared at the tops of her nipples with avid concentration, still clutching the half full champagne glass.

Louise saw her reach behind her back and unclasp the spangled bra, letting the cups sag a little. Like shy children her breasts remained hiding behind the sparkling satin until, with a triumphant smile, Gina lifted the garment right away and exposed her fine bosom completely. The man's groan of delight could be heard even above the music. He reached out with his free hand and pulled gently at her long, distended nipples. Then he stroked her right breast and squeezed it a few times.

Louise was practically on the edge of her chair, imagining how it would feel to be in her sister's shoes right now. With another smile, this time one of complicity, Gina took the champagne glass from his tremulous hand and dipped her finger in the bubbles. She pinched her left nipple, making it gleam with the wine, then repeated the process with the other one. At once the man leaned forward and took the nipple into his mouth, sucking the champagne from it vigorously. She poured a little between her breasts and it began to run in a narrow rivulet which he eagerly lapped up.

Laughing with abandon, Gina emptied the rest of the glass over her breasts and the man went crazy, licking and sucking at her abundant flesh like a man thirsting in the desert. Louise couldn't help giggling. She looked at Ahmed, who gave her a tight-lipped grin then said, 'You'd never believe what he's prepared to pay for the privilege.'

'Is that all he gets?'

'Yes. Gina won't do any more tonight. Although what she's got planned for the big cheese is a bit more exciting. That counts as a feelie too, but the word covers a multitude of sins.'

Ahmed gave a strange dry laugh, almost like a cough, and lifted up the champagne bottle from the table. 'Some more of this, or has that spectacle put you off?'

Louise held out her glass and he filled it almost to the brim. She was feeling reckless tonight – and very horny. The spectacle of so much uninhibited behaviour was catching. A part of her wanted to kick off her shoes and dance on the tables too, with or without her clothes. How wonderful it would be to perform for the whole room, to have all those men cheering and whistling just for her!

Surprised by her sudden streak of exhibitionism, Louise turned back to her sister. The man had evidently had his share because Gina was coming down from the table and taking his face between her breasts for one last, voluptuous squeeze as the waiter hovered, ready to take the screen away. She was laughing and smiling all the way back to the stage door, but as she passed Louise's table she gave her a wink.

'Do you want to go and talk to her?' Ahmed said. 'She has about ten minutes before her next performance.'

'Okay.'

Ahmed led her through the door and into the dressing-room where Gina was leaning over a basin washing her breasts with scented soap. 'Oh hi!' she grinned, turning round as they entered. 'Won't be a tick.'

Louise found it strange that she had reverted to her everyday self so quickly. She seemed no more fazed by what she had just done than if she were taking a break from a supermarket checkout. She sat waiting on a chair until her sister was ready to talk.

'Well what did you think of that little exhibition, Lou? Not so bad really, was it?'

'No, it seemed very quick really. Once you'd got your top off, I mean.'

'Oh, he was well on the way by then. In fact, I think he probably came when I poured the champagne over my tits. Kind of sympathetic magic, wouldn't you say?' She giggled.

'You talk about it so . . . ordinarily. But I thought you were very good. I admire your . . . artistry, I suppose you'd have to call it.'

'Artistry, I like that.' She threw the back of her hand across her forehead, striking a dramatic pose. 'My dear, how I suffer for my artistry!'

'Don't make fun of me. I'm trying to pay you a

compliment without sounding too daft.'

'There's nothing to it, honestly, Lou. A few wiggles and a bit of teasing and they're happy as Larry. You could learn to do it. Any woman could, given the right coaching.'

'Maybe.' Louise sounded doubtful. 'But you have to have the nerve, don't you? To carry it through in front of all those men, I mean.'

'I can just about remember my first time. I was terrified, I admit that. But you know what saved me? I imagined them all as little puppy dogs that needed training! You're their mistress, I told myself. If they step out of line you must tap them on the nose, but if they're good little chaps you can reward them with a titbit. And, do you know, it worked a treat!'

Ahmed put his face round the door. 'It's Shamooz next,' he reminded Gina. 'So you mind you pull out all the stops. We want to turn him into a regular customer.'

'Have you put him in the hot seat?'

'Jerry's moving him there right now.'

Gina turned to Louise. 'The hot seat is the only private one in the club,' she explained. 'That's where we do the really intimate stuff for our top clients. I'm afraid you won't be able to see what's going on from where you're sitting, but Ahmed will take you into the office and you can watch from there.'

'From the *office*?'

Ahmed gave a cunning little grin. 'Closed circuit camera. We have to keep a watch on our clients somehow, especially when they're in the hot seat. If anything untoward happens and a girl loses control of the situation I can send someone in straight away.'

Gina was doing a quick costume change. She put on a pair of black stockings and suspenders, but without knickers. Then she slid a red mini-dress over her head but wore no bra. She thrust her feet into high-heeled shoes and sprayed perfume down her cleavage and around her thighs until the dressing-room reeked of the not-so-subtle aroma. Seeing Louse's wrinkled nose she explained, 'It's Egyptian perfume, "Lily of the Nile". Clients adore it, but it's a bit overpowering for my taste.'

She blew Louise a kiss and flitted from the room. Ahmed held out his hand. 'Come on, Louise. You and I are going to watch a little peepshow!'

Louise felt her heartbeat quicken as she followed him into the nearby office. It had been one thing to sit with him in the other room, with all those other people there. But would he behave as impeccably behind the office door, with no one else around? What if he became uncontrollably aroused by the sight of his wife pleasuring that rich client? Would he make a play for her?

She began to wish that she'd stayed safely back at the flat, after all.

Chapter Four

THERE WERE TWO armchairs in the small office and a screen was placed high up in one corner. While Louise took her seat Ahmed pressed some buttons and a shot of Gina walking across the main room came up. Although the lighting was quite dim the lascivious looks of the men as she sashayed past their tables was plain to see. Some turned to see where she was heading and watched her disappear behind a partition at the far end of the room.

Ahmed pressed another button which evidently activated a hidden camera. A man was sitting there in the enclosure, looking around. His eyes lit up when Gina entered with a broad smile and a pert wiggle of her hips. They exchanged a few words but couldn't be heard over the closed circuit system.

Louise glanced at Ahmed who was sitting with his hands steepled beneath his chin, surveying the screen thoughtfully. 'This is a man we really need as a regular client,' he murmured, half to himself. 'He's just been posted to London for six months and if he likes the club there's every chance he could bring in some more clients.'

Louise said nothing, disliking the man's mercenary tone. Did he have to be so cold about everything? She didn't know how he could bear to sit there watching his girlfriend making out to all those men without being disturbed by the sight. On the contrary, he appeared to relish it. He's just a pimp, she thought. Yet Gina seemed perfectly happy with the arrangement too. It was all very strange.

The scene progressed, with Gina waving her body back and forth before the avid gaze of the man called Shamooz. He was dark and thick set, with squarish glasses behind which his staring eyes were magnified. Louise could see that he was wearing an immaculately cut suit and expensive-looking shoes. When he moved his arm she caught a glimpse of a stylish watch on his wrist and a flashy diamond ring. Again she found herself wondering just how much this little entertainment was costing him.

'Come on Gina, get on with it. We haven't got all night!' Ahmed muttered, as Gina turned her back on Shamooz. She thrust out her behind and slowly raised the hem of her skirt to reveal her naked buttocks. She waggled her behind at him, then let the hem fall again.

'Better give him a fondle soon, or he'll lose interest,' Ahmed muttered.

Louise felt more relaxed now she realised that all his attention was on the performance Gina was giving. He seemed to have completely forgotten about her. She sat back in her chair and watched her sister turn until she was facing Shamooz again. This time she began to unzip the back of her dress, letting the front fall to reveal the plump tops of her breasts. The man said something and she nodded, leaning forward until her deep cleavage was revealed. He reached out and felt her breasts for a few seconds before she whisked them away and turned her back on him once more.

Gina lifted her skirt and stood close enough for him to caress her smooth derrière. She raised her arms and the front of her dress fell down about her waist but the man was too absorbed in fondling her buttocks to notice. He half rose from his seat and kissed her back, but she frowned at him over her shoulder and he stopped. For a while Gina danced out of his reach, still with her back to him, then she began to turn to each side, giving him a glimpse of her bare breasts. The long nipples stuck out provocatively and Shamooz uttered a sigh. Although she couldn't hear it, Louise could plainly see his mouth opening and his chest heaving with frustrated desire.

At last Gina gave him the full frontal view he craved and for a while she lifted her breasts and played with her own nipples, getting him more and more aroused. Then she slowly came up to him and let him grab hold of them himself. At once he thrust her right nipple hungrily into his mouth while he grasped the other one, pulling her pelvis close to his face with his other hand as if he were afraid that she might dance out of his reach again. Louise could feel the sexual heat seeping through her body, making her tingle in all her secret places.

'That's right let him suck you!' Ahmed

muttered, glancing at his watch. 'But don't forget he s going to want more for his money than that.'

'Will she go to bed with him then?' Louise asked faintly.

Ahmed gave his short, sharp laugh. 'No way!'

'But what if he offered enough money, would she then?'

'We've already told him that Gina is unavailable for any out of hours activities. That will only make him want her more, of course.'

Again Louise was shocked by the calculating nature of the man, but it was hardly her place to criticise. The vision on screen was getting hotter as Gina shrugged the remains of the dress down over her hips and eventually let it fall to the floor in a puddle of red silk, exposing her naked mons. She had shaved her pubic hair quite extensively, stopping short of becoming totally smooth. Only a small dark tuft now guarded the entrance to her pussy. Still wearing her suspender belt and stockings she slowly moved towards Shamooz once more. By now the poor client could hardly contain himself and was literally on the edge of his seat, his hands suspiciously restless in his lap.

Gina stood with her legs apart, looking down at the man who had paid for the privilege of touching her intimately. Now he would get his prize. She took his hand and guided it towards her open crotch. Louise smothered a gasp of surprise as she saw Shamooz lean forward, an incredulous look on his face, and slip his finger between her labia.

Wiggling a bit to let him inside her, Gina began to squeeze her muscles and gyrate her pelvis. It was extraordinary to watch because whereas, normally, it would have looked as if he were in a position of power, invading her private parts, now it was quite the reverse. Gina was taking the man's finger and playing with it mercilessly, satisfying herself in the process.

'That's right,' crooned Ahmed. 'Give him what he wants, sweetie. Just enough to whet his appetite for next time, no more.'

As Louise watched the man's face contort with what looked like agony, Gina seized his head and held it against her stomach as he gasped and moaned, smiling down at him. Eventually he withdrew his finger and sucked on it with relish while she backed away, saying something with a smile. He grinned back at her, and she pulled the mini-dress down over her head. Then she took his balding head in both hands and kissed it, before leaving the booth. Shamooz sat there looking dazed for a while then adjusted his fly and stood up.

'One more satisfied customer – I hope!' Ahmed smiled. 'Do you mind if I leave you for a few moments? I have to talk to Mr Shamooz, make sure that everything was satisfactory.'

Louise sat back in her chair, feeling strange. She'd been indulging in various forms of voyeurism lately, but she was fed up with feeling sexy all on her own. With a weary sigh she reminded herself that being alone, and entirely responsible for her own life, was something she would just have to get used to now.

However, she wasn't alone for long. The door soon opened and Gina entered, gleaming with sweat, her body covered by a robe. She flopped down onto the chair that her lover had just vacated. 'Phew! There must be an easier way of earning a living!' she grinned.

'You said anyone could do it!'

'Absolutely right. But not everyone can do it *well*. And there was a lot riding on that particular encounter. The prestige of this place is built on clients like that.'

She lit a cigarette, giving a long sigh as the smoke issued from her lips. Louise said, 'But don't some of the men go too far? I mean, try it on.'

Gina pursed her lips and blew out a stream of smoke. 'You'd be surprised how little trouble we get. Must of our clients do seem to respect the rules. And of course there are plenty of men around to protect us if anyone does overstep the mark.'

'What you did, just then – do all the girls go that far?'

'Not unless they want to. It's entirely up to them. Some draw the line at any physical contact. Others are prepared to go all the way, and all shades in between. That's the beauty of the job – you're in control.'

'So I could just dance then, nothing more?'

'Well, you'd have to remove your clothes, obviously. But that's all.'

'I see.'

She made it sound tempting, but Louise was still doubtful. Gina had been doing it for ages, that much was obvious, yet despite her token protests she must enjoy the work to carry on doing it. While Louise didn't like to bring up the question of money, she couldn't help wondering what else the girls got out of it.

Gina's break ended abruptly when Ahmed reappeared. 'Ravi's getting restless so get your bum in gear. He only wants a table dance, but he's got two mates with him. Table nine, okay? But do a turn on stage first, get the old anticipation going.'

'Right.' Gina stubbed out her cigarette and gave Louise a quick smile before leaving the office.

'Okay?' Ahmed said. Louise nodded. He gave her a mock bow. 'You may go back to your table now, madame!'

She followed him back into the main room where they sat at the table with a 'reserved' sign on it. All over the room girls were performing for their clients, showing off their assets at close range, some on top of the tables and others on the floor or on a little podium. Every exotic dancer seemed to have her own unique style but they all obeyed one rule: maintain eye contact with your client. They were flirting and teasing them to the limit, making the men who had paid for their services feel special.

When Louise asked herself the question 'Are these women being exploited?' she had to admit that there was no evidence of that. They went as far as they wanted to go, they were protected both by the rules of the establishment and by the waiters and doormen, whose eyes were everywhere, ready to spot the first hint of anything untoward. The girls were made up to look beautiful, their scanty costumes enhancing their undeniably lovely bodies. The more Louise saw of what went on the less she felt she could condemn it as sleazy or degrading.

Still, there was a considerable difference

between being tolerant of others and practising the same behaviour oneself.

By the end of the evening Louise had modified her views about the Seventh Veil and she said as much to Gina and Ahmed as they rode home in a taxi. They seemed pleased, but were preoccupied with discussion of what had gone on that evening. It was clear that the club was central to both their lives, and they had little life apart from it. When they got back to the flat Gina made them all a drink and they sat around in the lounge. Although she was tired, Louise didn't feel ready for bed. Her 'normal' routine, the one she had been following for the past three years of her marriage, had been disrupted and it felt a bit like jet-lag.

'So, Louise, what are your first impressions of our little business?' Ahmed asked, his eyes glinting keenly at her as he sipped a Brandy Alexander.

'I suppose you provide a good service. High-class, I mean. The girls looked very pretty and they were good dancers. And the men seemed very well behaved.'

'That's because they regard it as a privilege to be allowed entrance. We offer high-class entertainment and they pay a high price for it. To be a member of the Seventh Veil club confers some prestige.'

'For the girls, too,' Gina said. 'They can earn up to five hundred pounds a night, or more.'

Louise raised her eyebrows in surprise.

'Of course it depends on what service they offer. Those girls who are only prepared to dance probably earn nearer a hundred and fifty. But for the ones who are proper lap-dancers the sky's the limit. They're not only paid in cash, either. Sometimes they get gifts of jewellery.' She held out her right hand for Louise's inspection. A large emerald flashed on a gold ring. 'I got this from a client who became quite a friend. He left it to me in his will, bless his heart!'

Louise was stunned, and a little envious. Ahmed was watching her closely. He said, 'Aren't you interested now, Louise? You could pay off your debts in no time. Get a down payment on a decent new place.'

'I'd train you,' Gina said eagerly. 'From the look of you it wouldn't take long. You have a good figure and you move gracefully. Do you like dancing?'

'I used to.' Louise's reply was tinged with sadness.

'Well then, you'd probably enjoy it. And I think you could do with some fun in your life, as well as some cash. Tell me I'm wrong!'

'She might like to come to one of our party nights,' Ahmed said. He rose from his chair and Louise felt a slight tremor in her stomach when she saw where he was heading. 'We have a video you might like to see. . .'

He took down the box marked 'SV – Fetish Night' and slipped the video out. Then he frowned. He took down another box and examined its contents too. 'Gina, have you been looking at these?'

She shook her head. 'No. When would I find the time? You know how busy I've been.'

'In that case, how come they've been put back in the wrong boxes? You know how particular I am about that.'

He gave Louise a penetrating look. She felt her cheeks grow hot and knew that her guilt must be evident, which only made her blush all the more.

'I see!' Ahmed walked towards her, a weird smile on his face. 'You've been watching them, haven't you? While you were here alone and we were at the club. First you raid your sister's wardrobe and private drawers, then you make free with our video collection. What a mischievous little creature you are!'

Louise felt a flutter once again in the pit of her stomach that was half excitement, half fear.

She looked to Gina for support, but her sister had that same mysterious smile on her face. 'Yes, I think you've gone just a bit too far this time. You only had to ask, my dear. But helping yourself behind my back . . . well, we don't tolerate that kind of behaviour do we, Ahmed?'

'We certainly don't. But how are we going to make sure it won't happen again? I think we're going to have to punish her, don't you?'

Louise wriggled in her seat as Ahmed came far too close for comfort, perching on the broad arm of the sofa. 'What do you mean?' she asked faintly.

'Don't worry, it won't take long. Gina and I favour the "short, sharp shock" approach, don't we, darling?'

'We certainly do!'

Gina got up and went to open a drawer. She took out a small, supple cane and Louise gave a gasp of dismay. 'Oh no! You don't intend to use that on me, do you?'

'That's exactly what we intend.' Ahmed's smile

broadened. 'Stand up, like a good girl.'

'But this is ridiculous. I'm not in school now!'

'Unfortunately, as you know, caning is no longer allowed in schools,' he said. 'Personally I think that's a bad thing. Fortunately it's still permitted between consenting adults in private.'

'But I haven't consented.'

Gina flexed the cane with a smile. 'You will when you know the alternatives. I cannot tolerate the taking of liberties and you have taken several in the short time you've been here. Either submit to punishment, as a symbol of your determination to keep out of trouble in future, or you'll have to leave, first thing tomorrow. The choice is yours.'

Louise looked from one to the other in horror. They were talking in a tone and language that she could hardly decode. If this was a game it was a game of bluff, and she didn't know whether to risk calling theirs or not. Nervously she rose from the chair and watched as Gina handed Ahmed the cane then came up to her.

'Let me help you, Louise. I promise it will all be over before you know it, and it won't hurt – much. Now lift up your dress, which I must remind you is actually *my* dress, you ungrateful hussy.'

'No, Gina, this is quite ridiculous. I. . .'

'You know the terms, Louise.' Ahmed said sternly. 'And the more you prevaricate, the more strokes of the cane you will receive. Now hurry up and do as you're told.'

She could tell he meant it. As she hesitated, Gina lifted up her dress for her and summarily pulled down her panties. Louise didn't resist, not even when she was made to bend over and brace herself against the arm of the chair. She tensed her buttocks as Ahmed went to stand behind her while Gina looked on with amused approval. A deep embarrassment seized her and she closed her eyes.

Yet behind her apprehension Louise felt her pulse fluttering wildly and knew that, at some basic level, she was perversely enjoying it. Humiliating as it was to bare her behind to a man she hardly knew, it seemed trivial compared to what she had witnessed at the *Seventh Veil*. And surely he would not hurt her, would he? A few light taps were the most she expected.

So it came as a shock to hear the loud swish of the cane as it descended and to feel the sharp sting as it made contact with her vulnerable flesh. She winced and contracted her buttocks. Ahmed gave her another stroke, and then another until Louise felt her behind begin to smart horribly. 'That's enough, surely!' she pleaded, hearing the cane being raised again.

'That is for us to decide, not you,' Gina told her. 'Another three, I think, Ahmed.'

'I agree. Three more should be sufficient for a first offence.'

Louise tensed her behind as the next torment came and the next, keeping her cheeks as taut as possible until he had finished. She remained there trembling, tears springing in her eyes at the pain, but just as she was about to pull down her skirt her sister said, 'No, wait Louise. I'll get something to make you feel better.'

Out of the corner of her eye she saw Ahmed return the cane to its drawer then go and sit down again. He took up his glass as if nothing had happened, and resumed sipping his brandy cocktail. For a few dizzying seconds Louise hated him intensely, but then Gina returned.

'Stay still, I'll rub this ointment in,' she told her. 'It will soothe you.'

Although she wanted nothing more than to get to bed and bury her head beneath the pillow in shame, Louise submitted to the last indignity. The cream was deliciously cool after the heat generated by the beating, and soon she began to feel much better. Her sister's fingers were gentle, and the pain was already subsiding to little more than a tingle. A surprisingly pleasant tingle, she was soon to discover. When she drew up her panties and sat down gingerly on the chair again a feeling of warm satisfaction flooded through her lower regions.

'How do you feel?' Gina asked.

'Peculiar.'

'Don't worry about it, Louise. That was just Ahmed's way of finding out if you were into being caned. We have CP and fetish nights at the club, you see, on Thursdays.'

'CP?'

'Corporal punishment. Some of the English businessmen can't get enough of it. We get other types in too, MPs, judges. You'd be amazed.'

'Some like to beat, others like to be beaten,' Ahmed explained. 'And they'll pay good money for the privilege, too.'

'So whether or not you decide to take part in our other activities you might like to consider that,' Gina said.

Suddenly Louise felt terribly tired and confused. She gave a yawn then said, 'I . . . I don't know. I need time to think about it.'

'Take all the time you want,' Ahmed smiled, rising to his feet. 'I'm going to bed now. Good night.'

He threw Gina a meaningful glance and Louise realised that she was keeping the lovers apart. She rose too, and went to use the bathroom. Looking in the mirror as she scrubbed off her make-up, she couldn't help wondering whether she would be able to face herself in the mornings if she took up Ahmed and Gina's offer of work. Her hazel eyes looked back at her candidly and her full lips gave a little sexy pout, just to see if she could do it. She grinned then began brushing her teeth.

The following day she was struck once again by the atmosphere of gloom and doom in her office, but now she experienced it in contrast to the 'workplace' she had visited the night before. Her impression of *Seventh Veil* had definitely been of job satisfaction for the workers, not to mention all those satisfied customers! At Newbolt & Co, however, it was quite the opposite. The work was boring, the pay was bad and the prospects even worse.

In her lunch hour Louise made a quick tour of the employment agencies, just to see if there was anything better available. But there wasn't, and by the time she returned to the office she felt more depressed than ever. The rumours were still flying around but now they had escalated beyond selected redundancies to include the whole firm going bankrupt!

How marvellous it would be to just give in her

notice now, to walk out on the whole damn lot of them. If she decided to take up Gina and Ahmed's offer she could do just that. So why was she hesitating? Was she scared about what Martin would think of her?

It came as a shock to realise that she was. But why should she care, now that he had ruined their marriage? She no longer loved him, and what she did with her life from here on was entirely up to her. The debate raged off and on in Louise's head all afternoon and she was no nearer to solving it by the time she left the office.

But as she travelled back to Holland Park she started to feel differently. Far from being worried about what Martin might think she actually started relishing the idea of shocking him. Seeing what went on at the club, both live and on the video, had opened her eyes to how other men and women behaved, what they enjoyed doing, and it left her own past love-life looking pretty feeble. Why shouldn't she be more adventurous, for a change?

So when she arrived back and her sister enquired about her day, Louise surprised herself by replying, 'It was lousy. So lousy I've decided to take up your offer and work at the club. But I won't give up the day job. Not just yet, anyway.'

Gina gave her a warm hug. 'I'm so glad. You won't regret it, I promise you.'

'Shall I come along tonight, then?' Louise asked.

She was disconcerted when her sister said, 'No, not tonight. Why don't you phone in sick tomorrow and we'll go shopping and buy you some clothes, get your hair done and put you through a few dance routines. But tonight you need to rest. You look washed out.'

'Do I?' Louise sighed. It was hardly surprising. She'd had more excitement in the past few nights than in the past few years. This was life in the fast lane, but it would take some getting used to.

'But mind you behave yourself when we leave you alone tonight!' Gina grinned. 'Tell you what, I've got a dance video somewhere. Why don't you use that to limber up a bit, if you have the energy?'

Louise did as she was told and thoroughly enjoyed herself, prancing about like a go-go dancer in one of the clubs she used to frequent before she met Martin. In the good old days, she thought wryly. She went to bed exhausted at eleven and slept through soundly until eight the next morning.

Feeling only slightly guilty Louise phoned the office and told them she had a migraine. She wished she had the confidence to give in her notice, but it was too soon. What if she got cold feet and couldn't go through with being a table dancer? Then she would have burnt her boats. It only emphasised how different she felt from Gina, who had walked out of their house at sixteen with no money, no job and nowhere to go. Now look where she'd got to!

They set out around ten and went straight to Soho, where Gina generously provided her sister with several appropriate outfits for her new career. After a pub lunch she took Louise to see Dino, her own hairdresser.

'You hair could take lightening,' he announced when she was in his salon with a towel around her shoulders, a sitting target. 'Your skin will tone nicely, and I think you'd look great as a blonde.'

'A blonde!'

Dino and Gina grinned.

Louise opened her mouth to protest, but then shut it again. What was the point of telling herself she should live more adventurously if she balked at every new thing? She would go with the flow, see where it took her.

Even so, she was very startled when she first saw her new self in the mirror. The golden halo made her eyes look very green – and her eyebrows very dark.

'It suits you,' Dino assured her. But then he would say that, wouldn't he, Louise thought.

'You'll need new make-up,' Gina told her. 'I can help you with that. And we'll get your brows lightened a bit too. Soon no one will know you weren't born blonde.'

'Except when I take my clothes off!'

Gina smiled. 'Well, there are ways round that too.'

She'll be wanting me to have breast implants next, Louise thought grumpily as they travelled home on the Tube. But beneath it all she felt enormously excited at the prospect of her new life. In some magical way having a make-over was giving her more confidence so that by the time the crunch came it would no longer be the old Louise that was taking to the floor, dancing sexily and then removing her clothes. Maybe she should change her name as well!

Chapter Five

'I THINK "LULU" suits her new image perfectly, don't you Ahmed?' Gina was looking at her sister as she spoke, giving her a conspiratorial smile. Only the two of them knew that had been Louise's baby-name. Now it was about to resurrected as her working alias.

After a weekend of intensive training, Louise had shaped up really well and Gina was trying to persuade her lover that she was ready to appear at the club. Monday nights were always quieter, less intimidating, and she knew that would make her sister's first public performance less of an ordeal. She could do her five-minute dance routine and then be invited to perform before one of the regular clients, who were more likely to be tolerant of a nervous newcomer.

'It will do,' Ahmed replied, his black eyes narrowing as he took another professional look at Louise. She was going through her dance to the tune of 'Light my Fire', shaking her tight little butt and thrusting out her pert breasts with more abandon than previously. It wouldn't take her long to get the hang of it, Gina decided. Maybe they did share some wild strand of their mother's genes after all!

Louise flopped onto the sofa, looking exhausted, and Gina told her to make sure she got to bed early. 'You can come along tomorrow night and make your début,' she told her.

'Already? But surely I'm nowhere near ready yet!'

'This isn't the London Palladium!' Ahmed grinned. 'You won't be judged on your dancing ability – not much, anyway.'

'But I don't feel confident enough. Maybe I'd be all right on stage, but dancing at the tables where they can see me close up . . . surely that's far more nerve-wracking?'

Gina took hold of a spindly-legged chair and placed it next to a coffee table in the middle of the room. 'Okay, when you've got your breath back, dance for Ahmed. Pretend he's a client. Pull out all the stops and give it everything you've got.'

She went over and put the dance track on again while Ahmed went to sit down. Louise got to her feet, smoothing down the fringe of her bikini pants and straightening the straps of her bra. Gina made her go to the other side of the room and walk across to him.

'Fine, look him right in the eye as you cross the room. Be bold. This man has paid for the privilege of seeing your beautiful body. Show it off!'

Gina continued to watch critically as her sister sidled up to Ahmed and thrust out her spangled rump, proceeding to rotate her hips and thrust her mons upwards in a smooth rhythm. She felt oddly proud of her. The mousy little creature that had blushed and stammered when she'd been caught red-handed in her bedroom had been transformed into a sexually confident woman. On the outside, at least. What kind of sex-life she would have now that she was finally separated from that dork of a husband was anybody's guess. She would certainly have plenty of offers if she worked regularly at the club.

Slowly Louise removed the tiny bra and revealed her plump, pretty breasts. Gina saw the enlargement of Ahmed's pupils, a sure sign that he was titillated, and wondered if he was growing attracted to her sister. He hadn't shown much interest in her when she'd first arrived, but there was a certain vulnerable openness about her now that she imagined most men would find appealing.

The pace of the music increased and so did Louise's dance, her breasts jiggling up and down before Ahmed's intense gaze. She had her hands down the front of her panties now, teasing him before she took them down, and there was a definite erotic charge in the air. Looking at her face, Gina realised that Louise was actually enjoying it. Her eyes were a bright and seductive green, and her pink lips were soft and open as if ready to be kissed.

'She's doing it much better now, isn't she?' Gina said to Ahmed, going to stand by his chair and absently stroking his dark hair. 'Is she turning you on?'

'Definitely. If I were a client I'd want to touch her now.'

Gina put out her hand and felt his erection. She smiled up at Louise, who was inching the panties over her hips. 'You see? You're getting him really hard.'

At once Louise averted her gaze, her cheeks reddening. 'Maintain eye contact all the time!' Ahmed barked, making her freeze.

Gina tried to reassure her. 'He's right, Lou. You must keep looking at him, and carrying on with your act, no matter what. Don't let anything put you off. Try talking dirty to her, Ahmed. She must get used to that sort of thing.'

'I want to suck your tits,' Ahmed began, in a feigned gruff voice. 'And then I want to stick my fingers up you, back and front, and give you a good seeing to. Get 'em off, girl. Let me see what your bare bum and naked pussy look like, so I can imagine screwing both of them.'

Although Louise carried on with what she was doing, the smile and the air of confidence had vanished. 'Smile!' Gina said. 'Look as if you're still enjoying it. If you don't, how can you expect him to?'

Louise made an effort and the glow slowly returned to her skin and eyes. She was now completely naked and was stroking her own breasts, hips and thighs with sensual abandon, successfully ignoring the stream of words that was issuing from Ahmed's mouth.

'Good, that's very good!' Gina said. 'Keep looking at him and smiling, no matter what he says. He can't touch you, remember. Not this time, and never without your consent.'

At the end of the performance Gina gave her a hug. 'You did very well. And you're unlikely to have to deal with that sort of talk. Usually our clients are very polite, paying you compliments and making you feel good. I just want to be sure that you won't be fazed by anything.'

'I can't promise that,' Louise said ruefully.

Ahmed said, 'We'll make it as easy as we can for you tomorrow. We'll find some really nice guys for you, don't worry.'

Later, in the taxi on their way to the club, Gina asked Ahmed what he'd really thought of Louise's performance. He gave a slow smile. 'Well, she has a certain shy but brash quality, like a teenage virgin trying to be sexy. It's very appealing, actually. I'm sure that some of our clients will go for her in a big way.'

'Mm, interesting. But do you think she could ever be persuaded to go further?'

Ahmed looked thoughtful. 'I'm not sure. It depends how she's handled, and on her early experiences at the club. That's why we must be very careful. I've been thinking about who usually comes on a Monday, or who might be persuaded to come. There's Jojo, of course.'

'Yes, I thought of him. And Sirhan. He's good-looking, and very sweet.'

As the pair of them discussed various options Gina became quite excited. She was remembering her own early excursions into the world of exotic dancing, how timid she had been at the start and how very bold she had become since. It amused her to think of her little sister following the same path.

The following evening Gina found herself in a taxi again, this time with Louise beside her. Ahmed had gone to the club earlier to make the arrangements, and while they were alone Louise confessed to being horribly nervous.

'I'm so afraid that something will go wrong,' she admitted. 'Or that they won't like me or something.'

Gina gave her a sisterly hug. 'Don't worry, you'll be fine. I'll introduce you to some of the other girls and then you'll feel part of the team. Treat it like any other new job and just do your best. You'll soon feel at home.'

When they got to the club Gina took her straight to the dressing-room where Janice and May, a Chinese girl, were getting changed. It seemed a good idea for Louise to meet them, since Janice was one of the newest dancers at the *Seventh Veil* and May was one of the longest-serving.

'What number are you?' May asked her. She was referring to the number by which the girls were identified, and to which they would respond when any of the waiters held up that number of fingers.

'Number seven.'

'Ah, the luckiest number of all!'

Soon all three girls were chatting away and Gina felt free to go off and find Ahmed. She didn't usually work on Monday nights but often turned up at the club anyway, to socialise. Besides, she liked being near her lover. Seeing him from across a darkened room still gave her a thrill. She smiled as he gave her a thumbs-up sign from the bar and walked over to join him.

'Is everything okay?' she asked.

'Sure. Jojo's out of the country right now, but Ali and Sirhan will be here. So will Jules.'

'Jules!' Gina smiled. 'Ever the gallant Frenchman. He'll probably kiss her hand at the end and make her feel like a princess.'

'They all know she's a novice. We'll see how she copes with those and if anyone else asks for her I'll vet them. I've told all the staff.' He took Gina's face between his hands and kissed her on the lips. 'She's getting a really easy ride. I hope she appreciates it.'

'Oh, I'm sure she does.' Gina threw him one of her intimate smiles. 'And I do, too.'

'Well I'll think of some way for you to show your gratitude later!' he grinned, before drifting off again.

Gina offered her sister a brandy before she went on stage and Louise gulped it down. Then Janice took her hand with a smile. 'Come on, it won't seem nearly so bad once you're up and running,' she smiled, her blue eyes warm and encouraging.

Louise made a face, tweaked her costume, then took a deep breath. 'Okay, I'm ready.'

Gina watched them go then lit herself a cigarette and put her feet up for a few minutes. There wasn't much she could do to help her sister now – she was on her own. She remembered what her first night had been like: she'd almost wet her knickers with worrying. But the darkness had been her friend, together with the bright lights on stage. Looking out into the room all she'd been able to see was the dull glow of the table lamps, while the dazzling brightness that surrounded her had lifted her spirits, made her feel special. A bright bubble in a black void. Was that how Louise was feeling now?

After a while she sauntered through the swing

doors and joined Ahmed at the bar. From the back of the room they watched Louise going through her paces with the other seven girls, each of them dancing in their own individual style. She didn't look at all out of place. Turning to Ahmed Gina said, 'She's doing okay, isn't she?'

He shrugged. 'This is the easy part. We'll see what Jules thinks of her later.'

Gina looked over to where Jules was sitting, his eyes on the stage. She had danced for him herself. He was a sophisticated Frenchman but his tastes were surprisingly simple: he required beauty and innocence, or at least the appearance of it. And her sister had both in spades. Now he was beckoning the waiter over, a mere formality since he and Ahmed had already agreed terms.

The waiter held up both his hands, displaying seven fingers. It took a while for Louise to realise that she was being called and when she did she faltered momentarily in her routine but soon recovered. With slow deliberation she descended from the stage and began to slink her way across the floor to where the handsome Frenchman was sitting with his cigarette in one hand and his wine glass in the other, awaiting her arrival.

Gina joined Ahmed at a nearby table from where she could see the proceedings. Trying not to stare too obviously she nevertheless managed to glimpse her sister's swaying butt as she reached her goal and paused, giving Jules a long smouldering look. Good girl, Gina thought. She saw Jules smile faintly, taking in every inch of Louise from top to bottom and back again. Was he hoping that some day he would get more than just a strip-dance from her? Such a fantasy would certainly enhance his enjoyment of her performance.

The question was, would Louise be secretly reciprocating that fantasy?

Not tonight, Gina decided, she would be far too nervous. But that was what made all the difference between a dancer who was just a stripper and one who was really special. With a fond smile Gina remembered the first time she'd really wanted the man she'd danced for. He had been a young German student, brought along by his wealthy uncle to sample the decadent delights of his favourite London club. The young man's hair had shone a bright, beautiful blonde beneath the subdued lights, much as Louise's hair was shining at the moment. He had been tanned too, with sapphire eyes and a perfectly sculpted mouth. Even now warmth filled Gina's loins as she thought of him.

She had been working for Ahmed but had not yet become his mistress, Gina recalled. There had been no particular man in her life, yet she had yearned for that innocent youth with an indecent passion. Her dance for him had been sultry in the extreme, full of wild passion and libidinous implication. His uncle had seemed taken aback, as if he had got far more than he'd bargained for. She had offered the blond beast everything: her ripe breasts, her pulsating pussy, but through it all he had sat there remote and expressionless, making her want him even more.

Afterwards the uncle had lusted after her himself but she had graciously declined. Her purpose had been to inflame the nephew, that infuriatingly cold and distant young man with the pale cicatrice on his cheek that was his badge of courage. For weeks afterwards Gina had hoped that he might return, preferably alone, to sate himself visually on her charms and then to sample them in the flesh, but he had never come again.

Instead the uncle had returned, months later, on his next business trip. Gina had overheard him talking to Ahmed. 'That absurd boy!' he had expostulated in his thick German accent. 'He was mixing in bad company, you know, so I bring him here to make a cure. I think so many lovely girls, he will lust for them and be saved from his bad friends. The girl she dance like a dream, like Salome before Herod, but is he made hard? Not one bit of it, whereas I! Now he lives with a transvestite in Hamburg. Ah well, I try my best! You have a saying, how goes it? You may lead a horse to water, but cannot force the beast to drink.'

Gina smiled to think of it. But by then she and Ahmed had become lovers and her dream of the beautiful blond German had faded into oblivion. . .

'Look!' Ahmed whispered suddenly. 'Your sister is getting into the swing of it, I think!'

Louise had removed her bra and was dangling it provocatively in front of Jules's nose. He was regarding her with amused tolerance, as one might humour a child. All the same his eyes were fixed on her luscious pink nipples, hard as sugared almonds on the vanilla cones of her breasts. She turned her back on him and pretended to pull down her panties but then stopped halfway and flung her arms in the air, revolving slowly until she was facing him again.

'She'll have to perform a few more tricks to please Jules!' Ahmed commented.

'Oh, she doesn't have to do much. Not this time, anyway. Her amateurishness is what appeals to him. I remember him telling me how much he loved to see the new girls trembling and blushing through their routines, and how disappointed he was when they became slick and professional after a few weeks.'

Gina watched as her sister's taut buttocks appeared and she stepped deftly out of what remained of her costume, holding it coyly in front of her pubis while she turned back to face her client. Jules nodded and smiled at her. Encouraged, she let the last vestige of her modesty fall to the floor and the Frenchman gave her a spontaneous round of applause.

Some of the others in the room looked round and one in particular appeared very interested in Louise. He just kept on staring at her, and alarm bells began to ring in Gina's head. 'Who's that guy over there, in the blue suit?' she asked Ahmed.

He peered through the gloom, screwing up his eyes. 'Where? Oh, Mikey!'

'What do you know about him?'

'He runs a chain of casinos. I think he's only been once before. Tanya took him home with her as far as I can recall.'

'He seems very interested in Louise.'

'Good.'

'No, Ahmed, you don't understand. . .'

But he was already on his feet, going off to greet a regular. Gina turned back towards the room and saw that Louise had ended her show and was making for the exit. As she passed Mikey's table he reached out and took her hand, stopping her in her tracks. Gina stiffened, anxiously. But Ahmed had also noticed what was happening and was making towards the man.

Gina watched the men greet each other and then Ahmed sent Louise off backstage, engaging the other man in conversation. She got up and followed her sister through the swing doors, soon finding her in the dressing-room gulping down lemonade.

'How did it go?' she asked. 'It looked fine from where I was sitting.'

'Oh God, I was terrified!' Louise finished the bottle and gave a little hiccup. 'Honestly, Gina, I don't know where I'll ever find the nerve to go through that again.'

'Nonsense! The first time is always the worst. Give yourself a rub down with cologne. I find that a marvellous tonic. Then you'll be ready to meet Ali. He's a nice chap, you'll like him.'

'Someone stopped me on my way out,' Louise said, her eyes wide with apprehension. 'He said he wanted me to do something for him. I've no idea what he meant. I don't think he speaks English very well.'

'Don't worry, Ahmed will sort it out. If he decides the man is too demanding he won't let you dance for him. You can trust him.'

She left Louise spraying herself with cologne and went back to the bar, where she found Ahmed talking to Jules. The Frenchman kissed her hand with his dry lips as she joined them, saying, 'Your sister is quite charming, Gina.

Where have you been hiding her all this time?'

'She's only my half-sister. We lost touch for a while, but I shan't let that happen again.'

'It is good to see her following in the family tradition! Will she progress, do you think?'

Gina knew at once what he was hinting at. 'For the moment she's content to dance, Jules. And I shan't push her. She must find her feet in her own way, and in her own time.'

'And very pretty feet they are too,' he murmured. 'Oh look, she has come back on stage. Now we are in for another treat, I think.'

For a while Gina watched her sister, then she saw Ali arrive. He waved her over.

'So, I am to have the pleasure of your sister's company tonight?'

'Yes, Ali. Be nice to her. It's her first night.'

'Ah, you make her sound like a virgin on her wedding night.'

Gina laughed. 'Dream on, Ali!'

They both watched as Louise gyrated on stage, her slender waist swaying and her stomach undulating as she moved her pelvis. Mikey, the casino tycoon, lit a fat cigar and leaned back in his chair, watching her through narrowed eyes. Although she tried to remain objective about the clients, Gina didn't like him much. There was something arrogant about him, something corrupt, as if he thought he was above the law. She reminded herself to get a profile on him from Tanya sometime.

When he snapped his fingers at the waiter Louise gave a startled look in his direction and Gina was instantly alert. The waiter held up seven fingers and Gina held her breath. When Louise began to descend from the stage she hurried to Ahmed's side.

'No, Ahmed! She mustn't dance for him,' Gina whispered urgently. 'Only for the clients we arranged. Go and stop her.'

'It's okay, she can give him what he wants. The man's hot for her, and if she dances for him tonight he'll come back tomorrow.'

'But I don't trust him. She's too inexperienced. Let her dance for Ali now instead.'

Ahmed turned away from her, his face hard. Gina knew better than to tackle him in that mood. She said nothing more, only watched the scene unfolding before her in helpless suspense. Her sister had reached Mikey's table now and was beginning her naive little dance, but already he was reaching out and trying to touch her, his strong fingers grasping eagerly at the flying fringe on her tiny briefs.

'My turn next?' Ali enquired pleasantly.

Gina shrugged. 'Who knows? Ask Ahmed.'

She was angry with her lover, very angry. It was important to give her sister an easy ride on her first night, but that Mikey character could prove to be a loose cannon. Gina saw Ahmed chatting to another client with his back to the stage, ignoring what was happening with Louise. Mikey made a grab for her and one of the waiters hovered uncertainly, but then Louise twirled round and almost bumped into the man's chair.

A stream of obscenities could be heard throughout the room. Louise paused, her face pale and strained, wondering what to do. Gina took a few steps towards them but then her sister pulled herself together and forced a smile. She resumed her dance, but Mikey was sitting there with a face like thunder, his arms petulantly folded across his chest. Gina looked at Ahmed: he was still absorbed in conversation, ignoring what was happening in the rest of the room. Her anger grew and she turned to Ali for sympathy.

'Ahmed should never have let her dance for that man!' she said in an undertone. 'I don't know how he got talked into it.'

'Money talks, my dear, you should know that by now.' Ali took her hand and squeezed it briefly. 'Never mind, when it's my turn to enjoy your lovely sister I shall make her feel like a queen!'

Gina threw him a grateful smile. 'I'm sure you will, Ali dear.'

Louise had removed her top now and was holding up her breasts for Mikey's inspection but he was muttering under his breath at her. Even so his eyes were on her nakedness, feasting gluttonously. This is the first and last time she performs for him, Gina vowed to herself. She went to sit at a vacant table near to where the dance was taking place. If no one else was going to look after her sister she'd have to do it herself.

Now that Gina was within a few yards of Mikey, his vulgar comments were audible.

Louise continued bravely, starting to roll down her pants but taking her time. She had closed her eyes now, presumably to blot out the vision of his lecherous face, but he took umbrage, swearing at her to look at him. She stared back like a zombie and continued her dance, stepping out of her costume and waving it provocatively at him.

Gina knew that it was only the approaching

end of her ordeal that was keeping Louise going. Her lower lip was trembling ominously and her eyes were moist. She longed to intervene, yet it was not her place. At the first sign of physical trouble a waiter would come to Louise's rescue, but as long as the problem was one of language and attitude nothing could be done. She caught her sister's eye and smiled encouragingly at her, but it only seemed to make matters worse. Louise looked as if she were about to burst into tears.

At last the dance ended, but as she bent to pick up her scattered garments Mikey reached out and pinched her naked behind. 'Ow!' Louise exclaimed. She backed away, fear and indignation written on her features. Swiftly Gina rose from her chair and went over. She took her by the elbow and began to usher her firmly towards the door.

'Come on, Lulu!' she said. 'Time for your break, I think!'

As soon as they were outside the confines of the club Louise began sobbing. Gina put her arm around her and led her into the dressing-room then shut the door.

'That beast!' she exclaimed through the tears. 'He pinched me, Gina! I wasn't supposed to let him touch me, was I?'

'Of course not. Look, don't worry about it. I'll make sure it doesn't happen again.'

But Louise was in a state. She trembled constantly and kept breaking down into tears. 'I can't do any more tonight,' she kept saying. 'Please don't make me go on again!'

'Okay, I'll take you home,' Gina said at last.

It was a disappointment to Gina. She'd hoped

to see her sister dance for Ali and Sirhan. Still, that could wait until another occasion. She knew that both the men would be tolerant. They had been attending the club ever since its opening and were now considered friends as well as clients.

As they rode back in the taxi Gina did her best to reassure Louise that she had done nothing wrong. The fault had been with Mikey and, to a lesser extent, with Ahmed for allowing the unfortunate incident to take place. It felt a bit strange having to act as mother to her own sister. She was used to mothering the new girls, considering that part of her job as Ahmed's personal assistant and the most experienced dancer on the premises.

But now, as she put her arm around Louise, she was reminded of when they'd been girls together and a sadness overwhelmed her. At the time she left home she had been thinking only of her own future. It hadn't occurred to her that, in depriving Louise of an elder sister, she had been changing the course of her life too. Would she have rushed into that stupid marriage if Gina had remained to advise her? The guilt she felt about that was compounded now.

She thought that Louise would want to go straight to bed, but instead she wanted to talk. They chatted for ages, mostly about old times, and were still up when Ahmed returned from the club. He didn't look pleased. Almost as soon as he entered he took a twenty-pound note from his wallet and handed it to Louise with a scowl.

'That's your night's wages!'

Gina leapt to her feet. 'Ahmed, that's unfair!'

He turned on her impatiently. 'I don't think so.

She's lucky to get anything after the way she behaved.'

Louise seemed cowed. She thanked Ahmed for the money and started towards the door, but he hadn't finished with her yet. 'I hope you're proud of yourself!' he snapped. 'You let me down badly, both with Ali and with Sirhan.'

'It wasn't her fault,' Gina intervened.

But Louise stopped her. 'Yes, it was. You're quite right, Ahmed, I did let you down. And I'm very sorry. I let that man rile me, but it won't happen again.'

Gina snapped at Ahmed, 'See? You've put her off the whole idea now. You should never have allowed her to dance for Mikey.'

To her astonishment, her sister said, 'No, Gina, it's not put me off. What happened tonight has just made me all the more determined to succeed, that's all.'

Ahmed's face broke into a smile. He took Louise by the hand and led her to the sofa, where he sat down beside her. 'You see, Gina, your sister has spirit! I admire that greatly. The only way we learn is by making mistakes. The weak ones amongst us give up when that happens. The strong learn from them. And Louise has shown us tonight that she is one of the strong ones.'

Gina had to agree. Her sister's spirit was remarkable. But she fancied that she should have some of the credit in helping Louise get over her ordeal.

Louise began asking Ahmed questions. Mostly about how much she could expect to earn on a normal night. They hadn't discussed business in such detail before, since she had yet to sign a contract, but it was clear that Louise had now decided to take the job seriously. She wanted to know how hard she would have to work to earn the kind of money she needed to pay off her debts.

'You'd have to do at least ten clients a night to earn two hundred just from table dancing,' Ahmed told her.

'And for lap dancing?'

He shrugged. 'Maybe five, six.'

'And if I did the next thing, let them touch me?'

'You could earn up to a hundred per client.'

Gina saw a faint gleam in Louise's hazel eyes. Something had changed in her this evening. Far from being intimidated by her experience with Mikey she had become all the more determined to win through. Was it the spirit of revenge she saw mirrored there?

Chapter Six

LOUISE DECIDED THAT in order to do her job at the club properly she had to give in her notice at Newbolt's, so she did just that. She told no one there what she was now doing for a living. They were a part of her old life, the one she'd shared with Martin. In one fell swoop she had left it all behind, together with those dreary office clothes that were still languishing in her old wardrobe.

When she phoned her husband he'd asked, truculently, what he was supposed to do with her clothes now that the house was being repossessed.

'Get rid of them however you like, give them all away,' she'd told him.

'And the rest of your things?'

'I'll come over sometime and sort them out.'

She chose a time when she knew he'd be out of the house. For two hours Louise sifted through the debris of her past, finding surprisingly little that she wanted to retain. It proved a cathartic experience. Soon afterwards she rang her solicitor and instigated divorce proceedings. All of which was a great boost to her self-confidence.

Next time she went to the club she danced for Ali, Sirhan and four others besides, earning over a hundred pounds. It wasn't quite the riches she'd imagined but it was a very good start. The trouble was there were only three nights in the week when she could do it. The others were 'Theme Nights' and she didn't yet feel ready to join in the various weird goings-on. Still, if she wanted to earn big money she would have to move on, sooner or later.

But her libido was up and rising. Despite the fact that she wasn't getting any sex, Louise found herself becoming more and more randy as she relaxed into her new role of exotic dancer and became more expert at it. The dormant desires within her were being slowly awakened, and she was enjoying the process. After a particularly sexy session she would come home and make good use of the vibrator Gina had given her, needing to satisfy her urges before she could sleep.

She loved seeing the men getting all worked up as she teased them, especially if they were men who attracted her. And she began to dream of giving them a little more, one day. Then, one night, Mikey walked into the club again and Louise felt all her new-found confidence evaporating. The very sight of him made her shudder with loathing. Yet there was a weird attraction too, as if she and he had some unfinished business.

Louise did her best to ignore him but halfway through the evening Ahmed took her aside.

'Mikey was asking for you,' he began, and a

cold dread seized her. He grinned. 'Now don't worry. He wanted to apologise for upsetting you before. He says he was a very bad boy and wonders if you'd like to punish him.'

'What?'

Ahmed grinned. 'You know, like I punished you. Remember?'

Louise blushed. 'You mean. . .'

'That's right. Strictly speaking that should happen on one of our CP nights, but since he asked specially you could do it now if you liked. In privacy, of course.'

'I . . . I don't know what to say!'

'Either yes or no will do for now. If you agree, have a word with Gina and she'll help you organise it.'

Louise couldn't help smiling at the thought of getting her own back on Mikey. Her humiliating experience with him still haunted her, despite her success with other men. It would be good to get him out of her system. She nodded. 'Okay. I'll do it.'

'Good girl! Meet Gina in the office in ten minutes. She'll tell you exactly what to do.'

While she waited, Louise kept looking across to where Mikey was drinking and smoking his cigar. Now that she'd made her decision she began to look forward to thrashing his behind, making him whimper. If only she'd known that was his bag she would never have let him upset her before.

Gina was ready in the office with an array of whips. She made Louise practise on a cushion until she found the one that felt easiest to wield. It was a small, thick-handled one that made a satisfying crack when she whisked it through the air.

'You can get him to come in here if you like,' Gina suggested. 'Try a bit of role-play.'

'How do you mean?'

'Well, this could be the boss's office. You could be punishing him for sexual harassment of a young female employee, or something. Use your imagination.'

Louise smiled. 'Okay. I'll try.'

Gina looked her up and down. 'You're not dressed for the part, though. Pity we didn't know about this before we left home, then we could have come prepared. Hey, I have an idea!'

She disappeared and returned a few minutes later with a dark green overall. 'I found this in the cleaner's cupboard,' Gina giggled. 'Put it on. Let's see how you look.'

When Louise was dressed in the overall her sister scraped back her hair into an elastic band and then found a pair of cheap sunglasses in the desk drawer. She popped out the lenses and handed them to Louise. 'Go on, put them on. Hey, that's not bad. Not bad at all. I'll go and tell Ahmed you're ready.'

While she waited, Louise felt a glow of arousal that filled her whole being and was one stage further on than sexual. She couldn't recall ever feeling quite like this before. In her life men had always been the bosses, the ones who told her what to do and made the decisions that she had to fall in with. She'd had to stand by helplessly when her father left home, when her husband gambled and drank away the mortgage, and when her manager had said there would have to be some redundancies.

Now she could reverse all her feelings of

helplessness with a few swift strokes of the whip. The prospect was intriguing. She began to plan how she would do it, and her excitement grew. Then she heard a sharp tap on the door and took her place behind Ahmed's desk, the whip hidden on her lap. 'Come in!' she called in a loud, stern voice.

Mikey entered, looking sheepish. He stood before her with his bald head bowed and his arms clasped in front of him. In a small voice he said, 'You wanted to see me, madam?'

'Yes, I certainly did!'

Louise placed the whip on the desk where he could see it and rose from her chair. She walked slowly round the desk, enjoying keeping him in suspense. Then she stopped about a foot away from him. She stood tall, throwing her shoulders back and her chest out, and at once felt a surge of real power go through her like an invigorating shock.

'You insulted me. What do you have to say for yourself?' she asked at last.

He raised his eyes a little, keeping his head down. 'I am sorry, madam.'

'Being sorry is not enough. You must be punished. Six strokes of the whip, I think. Take your trousers off and put your hands on the desk.'

'But, madam. . .'

'No arguments! If you don't do as you're told at once I shall double the punishment.'

Quickly Mikey took down his black trousers and bent forward, bracing himself on his arms. Louise decided she wanted to see more of his rump. She made him bend right over and rest his head on his forearms. Then she seized the elasticated waist of his Y-fronts and pulled it down, revealing his well-covered buttocks. She picked up the whip and raised her arm in the air, relishing the moment. Then she brought it down smartly.

Mikey yelled, and clenched his buttocks tightly. She lashed at him again and this time he groaned in resignation. Louise smiled to herself. How she would like to do this to Martin! The thought brought new satisfaction to her soul as she struck again, making his corpulent flesh quiver.

Mikey turned his face towards her. 'Please, madam, isn't that enough?'

'No!' she snapped. 'Not nearly enough. You insult me even to suggest it. Six strokes is the absolute minimum for abusing a lady, don't you agree?'

'Oh, yes! Certainly, madam!'

'All right. Now tell me how wicked and ungrateful you have been to take advantage of my innocence. Get onto your knees and tell me.'

Louise was amazed when he obeyed her without question. Another wave of exultation went through her as he began to grovel at her feet. 'I am a worm, madam, a worthless creature. I dared to touch your perfect body, and for that I should be punished most severely.'

'Quite right. So bend down with your face on the floor, as if you were worshipping.'

He looked so ridiculous with his great white moons stuck in the air that Louise had to stifle a giggle. Beneath his belly hung his insignificant genitals. She brought the whip down again. He moaned and prostrated himself further until he was almost lying flat.

'Two more!' she announced. 'But first tell me how unworthy you are to even be in the same room as me.'

Mikey played his part to perfection, telling her that she was as far above him as the sun was above the earth. He swore that he would never insult her again but only be her slave, if she would let him. Louise gave him his last two lashes and then kicked him with the point of her shoe for good measure. He stared up at her in abject adoration before hurrying to obey the order to pull up his trousers.

'Now leave me, you disgusting creature!' she said, throwing him a last look of contempt. He bowed out of the room backwards, hands clasped before him, as if from a royal presence.

While she was getting out of the overall Gina returned. 'That creep seems very pleased with what you did. I overheard him telling Ahmed that you were a priceless gem in our collection of jewels!'

Louise giggled. 'I enjoyed it. And I wasn't nervous at all. It just seemed to come naturally to me.'

Gina gave her a searching look. 'In that case you might. . .' She seemed to change her mind. 'But it's early days yet. I don't want you to take on too much at once.'

Louise enjoyed the rest of the evening more than usual. Her session with Mikey had evoked a new sense of her own power, which was extremely satisfying. She danced with greater confidence and was bolder with her clients. She found that she could imagine touching them, being intimate with them in ways that hitherto she hadn't dared dream of.

'You're coming along fine,' Ahmed told her as they went home together. 'Maybe you'd like to try lap dancing soon?'

'Don't push her,' Gina warned.

'Of course not, it's entirely up to Louise. Still, the offer is there whenever she wants to take it up.'

Louse wondered vaguely what the 'offer' was, but since she was rather befuddled by drink and very tired she let the subject drop.

On Friday night Gina told her that she would be going away for the weekend.

'One of our most wealthy clients wants to take me to Paris in his private jet,' she smiled.

'Lucky you!'

'Don't worry. I've worked for it. But I hope you don't mind being left in the flat by yourself. Ahmed will be there too, of course, when he's not at the club.'

'Oh no, I don't mind. I quite welcome it, actually. It will give me the chance to catch up with myself, to take stock. Everything seems to have happened so fast.'

It was true. In just over a month Louise had changed her life around completely and she still didn't quite know who she was. She had lost touch with her old friends, the house she used to live in had a 'For Sale' board outside and Martin had gone into a rehab unit. Sometimes, in the depths of the night, Louise felt very alone and scared by all the irrevocable steps she had taken.

On the plus side, she really appreciated being with her sister again. They were growing closer then they'd ever been. Not that they'd had much time to chat, but at the club Gina's friendly presence had made all the difference. And the few heart-to-hearts they'd had at home had definitely helped to heal old wounds.

So when Louise awoke on Saturday morning and realised that Gina was gone a wave of bleakness threatened to swamp her. She went into the kitchen and made herself a black coffee and some toast, then Ahmed sauntered in wearing his dressing-gown. Louise felt a tingle of anticipation strike her, making her feel self-conscious. It was the first time they'd been alone together in the flat. He sat down on the stool, legs apart, and Louise tried not to look at his lean, naked thighs.

'Well, Louise,' he grinned, 'what are you going to do today?'

'Oh, I don't know. I'll go shopping, maybe.'

'And tonight?'

She shrugged. 'Stay in and watch TV, I suppose. I could do with an early night.'

'I would invite you to join me at the club, but I'm not going.'

'You're not?' Louise stared at him, suddenly apprehensive.

'No, I'm leaving Karl in charge. I thought maybe you would like to come for a drink or maybe go to another club, in the West End.'

Louise felt nervous. It didn't seem right that Ahmed was asking her out while Gina was away. 'It's all right, thanks, Ahmed. I'd rather stay here.'

'Okay. Then let me cook you a meal. Something Middle Eastern.'

She squirmed on her stool, wondering how to get out of it. The thought of spending an evening in with Ahmed was unnerving, but she had no option. 'Please don't go to any trouble.'

'It's no trouble,' he smiled, his dark eyes subtly insinuating. 'I would enjoy it. It's not often I get the chance to cook.'

For the rest of the day Louise was out, looking for somewhere to live. She'd decided that she couldn't impose on her sister for much longer, but she knew that it was really Ahmed she was seeking to avoid. Somehow he made her feel decidedly uncomfortable. Was it because she secretly fancied him? Or was it just because she believed he was attracted to her? It was hard to tell.

After buying various papers and looking in some estate agents' windows she concluded that she couldn't afford to live anywhere in that part of town but must look in the cheaper areas: Shepherd's Bush, perhaps, or Earl's Court. The prospect of tramping the streets inspecting run-down flats and bedsits was depressing.

She just had to earn more money, and soon. Fortunately she was in the right job, she just had to pluck up the courage to take the next step. Lap dancing, the intimate contact between her crotch and the client's fly. She'd seen the other girls doing it and it didn't look too difficult, but it seemed to be on the other side of a hard-to-bridge gap in her confidence. Well, she would just have to overcome her scruples. At fifty pounds a time she couldn't afford not to.

Reluctantly, Louise made her way back to Holland Park. When she opened the door of the flat with her spare key a delicious aroma filled her nostrils and Ahmed appeared, waving a wooden spoon. 'Hi! I'm glad you returned now because it's nearly ready.'

She smiled, already feeling more relaxed. Ahmed offered her a drink and she chose Pernod. It made her think of Gina in Paris. She went through to her room and found some loose-fitting velvet trousers and a silky top to change into, then she went into the bathroom to freshen up before dinner. As she sprayed on some of her favourite perfume Louise asked herself just what she thought she was doing, preparing herself as if for a date.

She had no answer to that.

The meal was excellent, full of subtle spices and washed down with some superb wine. Louise enjoyed chatting to Ahmed about her childhood with Gina, what she remembered of it anyway. When the conversation went on to her unhappy marriage, however, she became quite tearful and put up no resistance when Ahmed put his arm around her on the sofa.

'Poor little Lulu,' he said soothingly. 'You've had a rough deal, haven't you? But eveything will be better now. You are enjoying your life with us, aren't you?'

'Oh yes!' She smiled at him through her wet eyelashes. 'It's marvellous being reunited with Gina again.'

'Well, we are happy to have you here,' he smiled. Louise thought how nice he looked when he was smiling. She liked the way his soft, black hair flopped over his forehead too. And there was something very attractive about his slight but undoubtedly masculine body. She could quite see why her sister had fallen for him.

'I started looking for a place of my own today,' she said.

'There's no hurry. At first, I admit, I wasn't keen on the idea of you staying here. But since you've joined our staff at the club it has been quite convenient, hasn't it? Are you happy about working there?'

'Oh yes, I am now. It took me a while to get used to it.'

'It is the same for everyone, even those girls who have worked as dancers before. We have a different way of working from other places. And a more exclusive clientèle.'

'Like Mikey?' Louise gave a cheeky grin, which he returned.

'Yes, even Mikey. He might be an old rogue but his ill-gotten gains entitle him to the same services as anyone else.'

'I've been wondering . . . about this lap dancing.'

'Yes?' Ahmed's mouth was very near hers now, making her feel dizzy.

She pulled away from him a little. 'I thought I might try it. Only I don't know exactly what to do. I've watched the other girls, but I'm still nervous of doing it myself.'

'Would you like to practise?'

Louise felt a dark thrill pass through her. 'What, now? On you?'

He laughed. 'Why not? I don't see who else you've got to practise on.'

'Well, I don't know. . .'

'There's nothing to it, honestly. You've already danced for me, anyway.' He got up and went over to the hi-fi system, selecting a CD. When he turned round his gaze was intensely compelling. 'Dance, little lady! Let go of your inhibitions and dance for me as if I were a client. Then you will come and sit on my lap and continue dancing!'

Slowly Louise rose from the couch and kicked off her shoes. It felt strange dancing in her clothes and soon she was stripping to her underwear. Her head felt muzzy and her nipples and clitoris were tingling inside her silky bra and drawers as she kept looking into Ahmed's black, knowing eyes. He crooned his approval now and then, keeping up her morale. Not that she really needed it. Dancing for him made her feel deliciously seductive and womanly.

At last, when she was wearing only her tiny silk pants, he beckoned her towards him. She noticed that he had taken off his shoes and socks. She slid onto his lap and he whispered, 'Now put your feet on the floor and slide up and down my thigh.' As soon as she did so he gave a groan. 'I think we'll make this a "feelie", shall we?' Without waiting for her reply his hands cupped her breasts, making her moan with arousal. The friction of his rough trousers on the delicate swelling bud of her clitoris was most titillating, and Louise found that she could alter the pace and angle of her movements at will, rising and falling as well as moving forwards and backwards.

Suddenly she ground her mons hard against his crotch and heard Ahmed groan again. His mouth fastened on one of her nipples, making her shudder. Locked into an ascending spiral of excitement Louise turned around and waggled her rear against the bulge of his fly, where his cock was evidently straining towards a climax too. His hands seized her breasts and his mouth gave a soft nip to her neck, making her squirm with ecstasy and throw her head back against his shoulder. 'That's the way!' she heard him whisper. 'Now we're cooking, no holds barred!'

It was only when his expert fingers found her clitoris that Louise realised the full potential of the new position. Her efforts became more frenzied as her own libido increased in leaps and bounds, taking her near the limit of her endurance. Between the twin cushions of her buttocks she could feel the hard prominence of his penis, now thrusting against her, and she had a definite urge to make him come. His nails were scratching delicately at her nipples while his thumb worked her clitoris in firm circles, increasing the erotic tension to fever pitch.

'I thought I was the one who was supposed to be doing all the work?' she said, gasping as she turned to grin at him.

'You're doing fine, just keep going,' he replied, his voice thick.

But she wanted closer contact with that secret weapon he held concealed in his trousers. Feeling it through his clothes was no longer enough, she wanted to see it, touch it, taste it. Abandoning all her remaining reserve she hopped off his knee and knelt before him, her erogenous areas still throbbing with desire, and went to undo his zip.

'You must charge more for this, you know,' he grinned down at her.

She returned his gaze saucily. 'Well, are you willing to pay?'

'Oh yes! Name your price, little lady!'

Louise slid the zipper down and proceeded to extricate the short, thick shaft from his underwear. She encircled its base with her thumb and forefinger, then bent her lips to the glossy pink glans. Ahmed's fingers continued to play with her breasts as she knelt there and soon she managed to manoeuvre herself onto his naked foot, where his big toe first played very dextrously with her clitoris and then managed to find its way right inside her.

As she proceeded towards a climax, with that wicked toe alternately invading her and rubbing her clitoris, Louise's enthusiasm for the act of fellatio grew. Soon she was sucking and swallowing at the shaft while she licked back and forth across the glans, her fingers cupping his balls within his pants. She felt them tighten and knew that he was on the brink of orgasm. A few last movements of her lips and tongue made him come, spurting wildly, and the sensation of his hot convulsions triggered her into similar excesses.

The sole of Ahmed's foot was stuck firmly between her thighs, his toes rapidly clenching and unclenching which was producing the most exquisite stimulation for Louise's pussy and rocketing her into one of the most prolonged and intense orgasms she'd ever experienced.

'Oh God!' she moaned gruffly, as the bliss went on and on. She was dimly aware of Ahmed collapsing onto the sofa and removing his foot from her crotch, but that didn't stop the amazing waves of sheer ecstasy. She wallowed in them, forgetting everything in her self-abandon, until the tide began to diminish and she became more aware of her surroundings in general, and of Ahmed in particular.

Scrambling up beside him on the sofa Louise curled up with her head against his chest, pulling open the bottom of his shirt so that she could feel the warm, hairy flesh beneath. His arm encircled her and she could feel his breathing slowing, becoming more regular. A deep and drowsy satisfaction filled her veins.

Some time later she came to and realised that she must have dozed off. She was alone on the sofa, with a blanket draped over her, and there was the sound of running water in the bathroom. Sleepily she got up and rescued her clothes, which were strewn all around. She took them through into her room and got into her dressing gown. By then the sound of the shower had stopped and Ahmed was emerging.

Louise blushed as she remembered what they had done together. She had now gone through all the delights on offer at the *Seventh Veil* with Ahmed. Whether she could go through those same acts with a complete stranger only time would tell.

'Louise!' he smiled, his face lighting up as he saw her. 'You fell asleep.'

'I know.' She gave a yawn. 'Suppose I'd better get to bed.'

He came up and took her into his arms. 'I'd ask you to sleep with me, but I don't think either of us would get much rest tonight.'

She gave him a startled look. 'What about Gina?' she asked quietly.

'Oh, she wouldn't mind.'

'How can you be so sure?'

'Because we have an agreement. We're not bound to each other. We love each other, but that doesn't mean we can't have sex with other people.'

'Doesn't it?' Louise frowned in disbelief. She'd like to hear Gina's side of the story sometime. What they had just shared was undoubtedly a sexual experience, even if it had gone under the guise of 'vocational training'!

Ahmed seemed to read her thoughts. 'You don't have to worry about upsetting Gina. And I have to tell you that your technique is sensational! You can dance in my lap any time.'

Louise gave him a wry look and passed on into the bathroom. While she brushed her teeth she felt some of her former excitement return. Working at the *Seventh Veil* she had the opportunity not just to earn money through satisfying the clients, she could discover new urges of her own, and satisfy them too. Free to experiment with sex, she could explore her secret, inner world without shame. It was an intriguing prospect indeed!

Yet there was still a nagging voice that told her this was all too good to be true. Surely Gina would feel some degree of jealousy if she knew how her lover and half-sister had been behaving behind her back. It would be easy to pass it off as 'just practising' but in her heart Louise knew it had been much more than a mere rehearsal. After a while she had forgotten all about technique and followed her instincts. She had lost her detachment and become completely swept away by the feelings that had overwhelmed her. What they had taken part in that evening had not been a simulation but the real thing!

The next morning Louise stayed in bed until she

heard Ahmed go out, around ten, to get the Sunday papers. Then she dressed quickly and went out herself, going in the opposite direction from the newsagents. Try as she might to dismiss the episode with Ahmed as lightly as he appeared to have done, she couldn't help feeling horribly guilty. She would have felt quite differently if she'd been able to discuss it with her sister beforehand, or even performed for Ahmed in front of Gina, as she had before.

It was a pleasant morning and Louise took the Underground to Camden, where she and Martin used to browse around the market on a Sunday morning. She even recognised some of the stall-holders, but the familiarity was only superficial. The changes that had been wrought in her personality and lifestyle meant that she viewed the remnants of the past as if she were in a foreign land.

For a while she wondered about the old Louise: what had motivated her to stay in a loveless marriage for so long? Why had she been content to settle for less? However guilty she might feel about it now, the plain fact was that the sex she'd had last night with Ahmed had been fantastic. She felt her sexual education had only just begun, and the years she'd spent with Martin had been wasted ones as far as discovering her sensual potential was concerned.

Poor Martin. Going past the stall where they'd bought several knick-knacks for the house she indulged herself in sentimental regret for a few minutes. Then she pulled herself together. It was time to go back to the flat and discuss her future with Ahmed. She'd been staying there too long without paying rent. Either she should start paying her way, or she should move out.

And she also had to work out a regular schedule at the club. Now that her repertoire was enlarging she must decide which nights she would attend, which services she would offer, and what prices she could command. Fired by the thought that soon she was going to get her life in order, in a practical and financial sense at least, Louise strode out confidently towards the nearest Tube station.

Chapter Seven

THE WEEKEND IN Paris had been wonderful fun. David had taken Gina on a tour of the most disreputable night-clubs he could find, for a non-stop orgy of titillation. And she had been happy to continue on a more personal and private basis when they dragged themselves back to their luxurious hotel in the small hours.

But now she was glad to be home. As the chauffered Rolls dropped her off outside her apartment block Gina wondered what had been going on in there while she was away. Had Ahmed managed to seduce Louise yet? Maybe her sister was already feeling deliciously guilty, dreading her return and not knowing how to face her. She giggled at the idea. Poor Louise! She was so naive.

Louise was there alone. She'd washed her hair and was sitting in her drab towelling dressing-gown watching television. She started guiltily when Gina entered, making her suspect that something had, indeed, been going on. Smiling, Gina walked forward and gave her a kiss on the cheek. 'No, don't get up. I'll make some tea. Would you like some?'

'Er . . . no thanks.'

Louise looked edgy, her cheeks flushed. She glanced only briefly at her sister and then looked back at the screen. Gina walked into the kitchen, still smiling, made herself a drink then returned to the living-room. 'So, what have you been doing while I was away?' she asked.

'Doing?' Louise jumped like a scalded cat. 'Nothing. Nothing much, I mean.'

'Well, aren't you going to ask me if I had a good time in Paris?'

Louise flicked the remote to silence the set, then turned around. 'Of course, how rude of me!' Her tone grew warmer. 'What did you do? Where did you go?'

'Oh, we mostly explored the night life. Transvestite clubs, strip joints, sex shows. All the usual tourist sights!'

Louise giggled, but the strain was still there around her eyes. 'Were any of them like *Seventh Veil*?'

'One or two perhaps. Let's just say I picked up a few good ideas and inspirations. Where's Ahmed, by the way?'

Louise averted her gaze. 'I don't know. He had to go out. Said he'd be back by eight. He's not going to the club until ten, and he thought you might like to join him.'

'Did he go last night?'

'No, he didn't, as a matter of fact.'

'I thought perhaps he wouldn't. The pair of you had a night in then, did you?'

She saw the flush creep into Louise's pale cheeks again, proof positive that something had been going on between them. Gina sipped her tea thoughtfully. She would wait for her sister to tell her in her own good time. Because she definitely would, eventually.

'Ahmed kindly cooked me a meal,' Louise said. 'And we talked about my future in the club.'

'You did? What conclusion did you come to?'

The hazel-green eyes were looking straight into hers now. Behind the slight uncertainty Gina detected a new pride and optimism. 'He thinks I might be ready to try some lap dancing.'

'And what gave him that idea?'

Gina held her sister's gaze, willing her to tell her the truth. She knew Ahmed too well to believe that he'd simply had a conversation with Louise. She'd noticed the empty wine bottles in the kitchen, the dirty glasses. Most telling of all, she could sense a new defiance in the girl. It was written on her face as plain as day: yes, we did it, but what do you care, coming back from your dirty weekend in Paris?

She saw Louise take a deep breath. 'Well, we discussed it and he suggested that I might like to try.'

'Ah!'

She continued, very fast. 'So I did, and it was okay. He said . . . well he said my technique was fine and he thought I could manage to satisfy the clients. . .'

'Did you satisfy him?'

Louise looked scared. 'What?'

'Did you make Ahmed come when you wriggled in his lap? Or did it take a bit more than that to get him off?'

The scared look intensified. 'Gina, I didn't go to bed with him. . .'

Gina smiled. She was enjoying this. 'No, you

did it right here on the sofa, didn't you? What was it, a hand-job, a blow-job or did you, as we used to say, "Go all the way"? Come on, you can tell your big sister.'

Louise had her knickers in a twist now, all right. The look on her face was priceless. Gina knew she was being cruel, but she was so much enjoying seeing all that unnecessary guilt and suffering. One day they might share the joke. But for the moment she would savour the sense of power it gave her, this rare confrontation between her own free-loving lifestyle and the vestiges of her sister's moral code.

'Look, Gina, I'm really sorry. I'd had too much to drink last night and one thing led to another. But I didn't let him go all the way, honestly I didn't. It was only a blow-job.'

'Oh, that's all right then.' She's infused a note of irony into her voice, just for a tease.

Louise gave a rueful smile. Her blonde hair was almost dry and, fluffed up around her face, gave her an angelic look. 'I'm looking for somewhere else to stay. I think it's probably best if I moved out.'

'Why, because you got a bit carried away with Ahmed? Don't be ridiculous!'

'It's not just that. . .'

'Look, I know you can't afford a decent place yet. Why don't you build up your savings for a couple of months and then start flat-hunting? Besides, I like having you here. I'm in no hurry to get rid of you.'

Louise looked sheepish. 'I thought you would be, when you knew what had happened between me and Ahmed.'

'What, when I was having such a great

weekend with David? Look, Ahmed and I aren't possessive about each other, okay? We can't afford to be in our business.'

Suddenly Gina had a great idea. She gave a huge grin and plonked herself down on the sofa beside Louise, putting her arm around her shoulders. 'Hey, guess what? I'm going to give a party! Right here in the flat. We haven't had one for ages, and it will be fun to introduce you to some new people.'

She didn't mention her hidden agenda, which was to get Louise used to mixing with uninhibited types who were as happy in a threesome as in a couple, had affairs with both sexes, and who didn't mind what anyone else did as long as everyone was happy. Her sister had a few lessons to learn about the swinging scene before Gina could feel comfortable about her attending a Fetish Night at the club.

It would be fun planning another party at home. The club events were essentially business, with the clients paying for their privileges. This would be a chance to catch up with old friends and to experiment with new delights. Gina couldn't wait to tell Ahmed, sure that he would be as pleased as she was with the idea.

She told him about it on the way to work that night. 'I want Louise to meet more people, so I've decided to hold a party.'

Ahmed smiled. 'Good idea.'

'I gather you two have been getting better acquainted.'

'Of course. Wasn't that what you expected?'

'Absolutely. But you will treat her carefully, won't you? She's the only sister I've got.'

Ahmed kissed her. 'Don't worry, it was her

idea. Anyway, she enjoyed it as much as I did.'

'And you really believe she's ready to move on?'

'Yes. More to the point, she thinks so too. I'll tell Jules she's ready to give him a lap job tomorrow night. He'll enjoy that. When are you thinking of holding the party?'

'How about a week on Saturday?'

'Perfect. Now tell me what you did in Paris.'

Gina sat back in her seat and re-crossed her long legs. 'Well, the most thrilling moment was when we were at the *Boîte de Chatte*. They made what they called a *Cascade de Baisers*. It was a human pyramid – you know, like the 'Halifax' ads – but every row was kissing the row above in the most intimate places!'

'How on earth did they manage that?'

'They sat with their legs over each other's shoulders, boys and girls in alternate rows and each facing a different way. It was very ingenious!'

'I think that's a bit beyond us at the *Seventh Veil*.'

'Maybe, but it's given me an idea. . .'

For the rest of the journey Gina let her imagination run free. She was always the one to come up with the innovative ideas, while Ahmed thought of ways to put them into practice. It was the perfect patnership. On Sunday nights they often put on special shows, and Gina was always looking for new angles. The current *Showgirls*-style sexy ballet was wearing a bit thin.

All through the evening Gina kept taking time out to compile her guest list. The invitations would be designed by her arty friend Sara, who loved to draw erotic subjects. Gina's last party had been a great success and her friends were always asking her to give another. Well, she would surprise them all this time by introducing them to her kid sister!

First, though, Louise had to make some progress at the club. When Gina took her along on Monday night she sensed a new excitement bubbling away below the surface of those greeny-brown eyes. She wanted some tips about lap dancing, but Gina told her that she should follow her instincts.

'Just remember that the man's penis is your guiding star, so to speak. You should try to keep in contact with it at all times. And if he starts to lose his erection make sure you do something to get him excited again, even if it's only whispering dirty words in his ear.'

'Isn't it a bit messy when they come?'

'They don't always. Sometimes a client will want a lap dance to get him in the mood for a blow-job later. Or they might just want a bit of a tingle. But if they expect to come they generally wear a condom.'

Louise twisted a strand of her blonde hair absently around her finger. Her eyes were bright with anticipation. 'I think I'm going to enjoy this! Ahmed said that both Jules and Ali want me to dance in their laps tonight. Since I know them already I shan't be so nervous.'

'Some men are happy just to sit there and let you get on with it. Others want to touch you, but you should agree a fee in advance. Let Ahmed handle the money side for now.'

To Gina's surprise Louise suddenly gave her a

hug and a kiss. 'You're both being so good to me! I'm sure you don't treat all your new girls with kid gloves like this.'

'Maybe not quite so much. But we do like to make sure everyone settles in well. No point in having disgruntled girls working for us.'

For a while that evening Gina was too busy to take much notice of Louise. David turned up unexpectedly, wanting to be entertained in private. She was flattered that he'd come back to her so soon after their Paris jaunt and they spent an hour closeted in the Ladies. It was one of his little fetishes to enjoy making love on a toilet seat while other women urinated in the cubicle next door.

Returning to the club, Gina saw that Jules was already getting his lap dance and, from the look of him, enjoying it immensely. Louise was astride his thighs, her pert buttock's sliding back and forth to the tune of 'Future Love Paradise'. Every time one of her nipples neared his lips he would make a play for it, sometimes slyly catching it for a few seconds when she would pause and slide back from his lap with a reproving grin, telling him to behave himself.

Gina looked around the room and saw that at least half a dozen other clients were paying close attention to what was going on at table ten. She had a feeling that Lulu was going to be very popular – and very busy – over the next few weeks. Of course the novelty factor had to be taken into consideration, since every new girl caused a bit of a stir. But after a while things would settle down. She would have her quota of regulars, some passing trade, some new clients.

She would be doing some table and some lap dancing, and maybe, eventually, get to sleep with some of the clients she most fancied. But it would be a long time before she got to the stage Gina herself was at, where a client became more like an old friend and would take her on trips abroad with him.

Sighing as she recalled the long, winding road she'd taken to get where she was today, Gina went to join Ahmed. He grinned at her approach and nodded towards table ten. 'She seems to be the main attraction this evening!'

'Well she is managing rather well, don't you think? But then she's had expert tuition!'

They continued to watch in silence as Louise increased the speed of her movements. She was sweating now, red-faced, and clearly near to climaxing herself. Jules had his eyes open wide and his hands clenched tightly, staring intently at her firmly fleshed breasts. She held them together and, bending her head, licked down her exaggerated cleavage. Even from a distance Gina could see his thighs shuddering and hear her sister's gasps as she joined him in the ultimate ecstasy.

A spontaneous round of applause broke out amongst those who had been watching their progress. Gina gave Ahmed a wry grin. 'A veritable star in our midst!'

'I knew she would be,' Ahmed said quietly. 'From the first moment I saw her. There is one hell of a sensual woman, but she's not been given the opportunity to express it.'

'That stupid husband of hers!'

'Precisely. We shall just have to make sure she reaches her full potential now, won't we?'

Over the next few days Louise's burgeoning sexuality started having a subtle effect on Gina. It was as if, being half-sisters, they were sharing the experience in some measure. While it had all started with Louise learning from Gina, now the reverse seemed to be happening. Gina felt herself becoming almost innocent again, her senses re-awakening, and the old habits that she'd acquired over years of dedication to sexual gratification, her own and others', were now being cast off in favour of experimentation and discovery.

The most marked improvement was in her love-life with Ahmed. While Louise lay in the spare bed – perhaps dreaming of new pleasures, or pleasuring herself with one of her sister's toys – Gina found everything she did with her lover exquisitely fresh and exciting. They'd done a few drugs together, but this was different, better. Fresh and innocent as young love, the pair of them spent hours in simple positions and movements that once they would have scorned. And when she came Gina felt herself opening up more and more, attaining multi-orgasmic heights where each new peak of pleasure seemed to merge with the next. So that when the time came for the party she was at a level of sexual awareness such as she hadn't felt in years.

On the morning of the party she enlisted Louise's help to get the flat ready. She had bowls of condoms strategically placed, and her armoury of sex aids on display. There were videos for viewing in the bathroom, along with the massage oils. In addition she would throw open her wardrobes to anyone who fancied a spot of dressing-up, including, of course, Louise.

'Can I wear this?' Louise asked, holding up a long silky black dress. It was slit to the waist on both sides and had panels of sheer black chiffon over the breasts. Gina knew it would look fabulous on her sister. Probably even better than it did on her. She nodded, smiling wistfully.

While Ahmed slept, preparing himself for the rigours of the night, the two girls enjoyed getting ready together. After they'd showered, Gina washed and styled Louise's hair. She piled it up on her head and let just a few tendrils fall down about her face.

'It's good to start a party with your hair up,' she told her. 'Then you can look so much more debauched when you let it down!'

'Brilliant! I'd never have thought of that,' Louise grinned.

'Now for the dress. I suggest wearing just some black silk panties underneath and a matching suspender belt, with sheer black stockings.'

'I wasn't going to wear anything.'

'Some principle. Put them on so that some lucky person can take them off later.'

'Is there anything else I should do?'

'Apart from make-up, which I'll help you with in a while, you must choose your perfume carefully. Which one makes you feel most sexy?' Louise produced the bottle from her toilet bag. 'Good. Put it behind your knees, around your navel, between your breasts, inside your elbows and behind your ears. Then you'll float in a veil of perfume all night.'

While Louise put on her make-up base Gina got into her own party gear, a catsuit in paper-thin red latex that accentuated every curve and cleft of her body like cling film. The exciting part about her costume was the presence of camouflaged flaps that gave access to her erogenous zones at the flick of a finger. She painted her lips bright red and slicked gloss over them, then applied the smoky eye shadow and thick black mascara that she knew made her look like a siren.

'You look fantastic!' Louise declared, seeing her in the mirror as she lifted the mascara wand to her lashes.

'Thanks. No, let me do your eyes! They're going to look amazing. Trust me!'

Before Gina had finished the doorbell rang. 'Oh God, someone's early!' she moaned, rushing in to wake Ahmed. He had already showered and only needed to fling on his white pants and matching loose shirt to be presentable. While he answered the door Gina rushed back into the bedroom to put the finishing touches to Louise's make-up, straining to hear the voices of the guests as they came into the hall.

'Sounds like the Girl-Lees.'

'Who are they?' Louise asked. Thanks to clever shading her eyes looked a vivid green now without a trace of brown. Her cheeks were pink with excitement and her lips dewy and moist. I could fancy her myself, Gina thought.

'A bunch of Chinese transvestites from Soho. Cabaret act. They're all called Lee.'

She laughed to see Louise's pretty eyes almost pop out of their sockets. 'Oh, you'll see a lot of strange sights tonight!' she promised her.

The guests started arriving *en masse* soon afterwards and began helping themselves to drinks. Gina introduced Louise to a few people but soon she got caught up in the action and had to leave her sister to fend for herself. She was challenged to play 'hunt the sausage' by an old cross-dressing friend of hers, and soon found out that he'd had the 'op'. A spot of foreplay with a vibrator followed.

Then a couple of lesbians invited her to join in their bathroom frolics. They all stripped and began sloshing soap and water around until their bodies were slimy and wet. They were joined by several other men and women, some of whom liked to watch and others who took part in what was rapidly developing into a free-for-all. People crawled in and out of the slithering mass of bodies at random, enjoying the sensation of being caught up in a kind of human slush pile. While they were groping and stroking and poking each other two people stood at the door with camcorders, filming it all.

Feeling ready for something new, Gina squeezed herself back into her catsuit and went back into the sitting room. The place was jam-packed with familiar bodies being very familiar with each other. She was soon grabbed by Charles, who loved to lift up her 'cat-flap' as he called it and taste her pussy. They lay sandwiched on the sofa between two couples who were engaged in some heavy petting, while on the floor Ahmed was giving head to a sexy black girl that their mutual friend Yvonne had brought along. Gina reached down just as Charles began to flick his tongue rapidly across her hot clitoris and toyed with Ahmed's erection for a few seconds before her own orgasm took her by surprise.

Afterwards she lay back, recovering, and surveyed the scene of debauchery in front of her.

While almost everyone in view was engaging in some more or less erotic activity she was quite startled to see one couple standing in the corner, drinks in hand, merely chatting as if at a conventional party. She was even more surprised when she realised that the girl was Louise. But who was she talking to? Squinting through the semi-darkness Gina finally identified him as Rick Morley. He was a one-time porn star and they'd once been in a low-budget skin flick togther. She couldn't even remember inviting him.

There were some loud groans at her feet. She looked down to see that Ahmed was having his balls sucked by a woman with huge breasts. Another woman was rolling a ribbed green condom down his erection. Well, he was having a good time anyway! She rose and wandered into the kitchen where good use was being made of her dips, but no one was bothering to use the corn chips.

'Gina! Wonderful party!' someone gushed in a drunken tone. Hands were placed over her eyes from behind and two giggling women began to search for a way into her private parts, while the man – she thought she recognised the voice of 'Dirty' Harry – started whispering obscenely wonderful suggestions into her ear. It wasn't long before her nipples and vulva were exposed and her three eager assailants proceeded to have their wicked way with her while a fourth plied her with with wine.

Several more orgasms later, Gina staggered from the kitchen back to the living-room and was amazed to see Louise still in conversation with 'Rick the Dick'. She managed to fight her way through to them and slapped her sister on her silk-clad rump. 'What are you doing standing here yacking like a couple of party-poopers?' She grinned. 'Hi, Rick! Made any good movies lately?'

'I've given it all up, Gina,' he replied gravely. God, he has gorgeous eyes too, she thought. I wish I could remember what we did together in that daft film.

'What did we do together in that daft film?' she asked him.

'Oh, the usual, I expect.' He smiled indulgently at her.

'It might have been usual for you, but it wasn't for me. Not at that time, anyway. I was only in it for the money. I expect you were too. I mean, it wasn't any fun was it, standing there starkers in some draughty room with me having to fluff up your erection when all I wanted was a decent cup of tea. . .'

Gina paused, aware that something was wrong. There was a definite atmosphere, but she couldn't quite make it out. Both Louise and Rick were standing there patiently, as if they were humouring her. Had she said something out of order? She mentally reviewed the conversation. Seemed pretty normal to her. Then she worked it out. She was excess baggage, not wanted on voyage, *persona non grata*. In short, she was playing gooseberry.

'Er, I've got to see a man about a condom,' she muttered, backing away. 'Have fun. Byee!'

'Extraordinary,' she murmured as she slid through the crowd. Someone caught her round the waist and began kissing her passionately. 'Oh Dave, I never knew you cared!' she grinned when he let her get her breath back.

Dave was wearing his karate kit. 'Ever done it

in the Teh-Khwang position?' he enquired. She shook her head. 'Want to try? It confers great strength. Heaven below, thunder above.'

'Try Alka-Seltzer!' she giggled, and moved on.

Returning to the sofa, Gina sat down and Ahmed fetched her a glass of wine. He sat beside her and began to caress her right breast through the open flap. She sipped her wine contentedly, drinking in not only the alcohol but also all the sights, smells and sounds around her. She felt like a bubble of calm in a whirlpool of sexual activity. The Girl-Lees were giving blow-jobs to all comers; three lesbians were making love with frantic energy while someone filmed them; Angus was taking Pauline from the rear while she pleasured another woman with a dildo; Claudia was giving Sal a lesson in fellatio on a banana. . .

'Great idea!' Ahmed smiled, bending to kiss her exposed nipple. 'Another one of your successful society balls I think, Lady Gina.'

But as her eyes skimmed about the room, growing jaded at the sight of so much flesh, so much dissipation, so much blatant exhibitionism, Gina was suddenly shocked by encountering the most erotic sight of all. There, still in the corner and still talking, were the two people who were oozing the most sexual electricity in the room, despite the fact that they weren't touching at all. For a moment Gina felt infinitely sad, and terribly envious. In a split second of intuition she realised they were sharing something that no other couple at the party was experiencing: the lightning flash of an overwhelming attraction for each other.

But the next time she looked towards that corner they had gone.

Chapter Eight

LOUISE HAD BEEN feeling a bit like a wallflower at the party before Rick came along. The people that Gina had introduced her to wanted her to join them in a blindfold session in the bedroom but she hadn't felt ready for that. She'd wandered into the kitchen to get herself a drink and found two women doing disgusting things with the avocado and cream cheese dip, so she grabbed a glass of wine and went back into the living-room. It didn't take long for her to feel out of place there, too.

She just wasn't used to having sex with strangers in such a random way. It was one thing to be doing it in the club, where there were rules and people to enforce them, but quite another to join in some freaky orgy with people she didn't particularly fancy. Maybe she wasn't drunk enough. Louise finished her wine and started to head back to the kitchen for a refill. Before she could get there, however, Rick appeared.

'Would you like some more wine?' he smiled at her, his handsome face appearing like a beacon of light in the darkness. 'I was just going to get some myself.'

'Thanks, I'd love some.

Their fingertips touched as he took her glass, sending a spasm of pleasure up her arm to her neck, from where it ricocheted down her spine. That was when she realised he was someone special. She awaited his return in a warm glow of anticipation. When his face loomed once more out of the steaming mass of bodies all around Louise felt her heart leap in her chest.

'There you go. Hope it's drinkable. Cheers!'

He had dark brown curly hair and startling blue eyes with long, sweeping lashes. His nose was straight and quite narrow, but his mouth was very generous. Louise couldn't take her eyes off his lips. They were broad and looked dewy soft, and he had a simply gorgeous smile. She wanted him to grin like an idiot at her forever, showing off those strong white teeth and filling his eyes with dancing light.

'My name's Rick, he told her, and she murmured hers in return. 'Hi, Louise. Are you a friend of Gina's?'

For some unknown reason she didn't want to admit kinship. 'Sort of,' she smiled.

'And I'm sort of an ex-colleague. We did some filming together, quite a while back now.'

Knowing Gina, Louise had a pretty shrewd idea of what kind of film that would have been. But again she had the urge not to go into it. There was no way she could explain her reticence, except that she was feeling strangely protective of this fragile new friendship.

'What are you doing now?' she asked, somehow

sensing that was a safe question.

'Mostly modelling assignments.'

'I can see why!' Rick actually blushed! It endeared her to him even more. 'What have you done recently?'

'Well, I'm in *Arena* magazine next month. Modelling men's clothes.'

Instinctively she took note of what he was wearing: a pale blue sweatshirt that emphasised the strong curvature of his chest, loose-fitting linen trousers and the latest in trendy trainers. He held himself with the casual grace of someone used to displaying his body, and she began to wonder what he looked like under his clothes. A buzz of excitement travelled along her veins at the thought.

When Gina came up and began her brief, brash conversation with him Louise felt the warmth of their earlier contact slip away and a jealous coldness took its place. She tried not to give in to it, but she was terribly afraid that the spell might be broken.

So when her sister moved off again and Rick turned back to her with another of his dazzling smiles she felt greatly relieved. 'So you used to work with Gina. . .' she began, for want of anything else to say.

'Let's not talk about work, past or present, yours or mine,' Rick said firmly. 'What do you think of this wine? It's Californian. I was there just last month, drinking this very same tipple in a bar overlooking Fisherman's Wharf.'

They chatted on about places they'd visited, places they'd like to visit, and soon Louise felt as if she was talking to an old friend. Sometimes she became aware of what was going on around them and it seemed unreal, like a movie set. But mostly Rick held her attention one hundred per cent, his blue eyes searching hers with an acute sensitivity to her mood. He smiled often, irresistibly, and made her laugh too. Although she didn't give it much thought, Louise knew that the attraction between them went far more than skin deep.

At last he noticed her empty glass again. 'Would you like some more wine?' he asked, his voice so low that she had to lean towards him to hear it through the hubbub of voices, laughter and background music. She hesitated. Something in his tone suggested he might have an alternative in mind. 'Well. . .'

'I'm enjoying talking to you so much, Louise. But obviously this isn't the best place. Why don't we find somewhere quieter?'

'I don't think Gina thought about having a quiet room.'

'No, but I've got one. And it's only ten minutes' drive away. How about it?'

She understood that he was inviting her to his place, and knew what that might mean when they gave in to the physical imperative. But it was years since she'd felt such an overwhelming attraction to a man. Rick was drop-dead gorgeous, but he was sweet too, and funny, and warm. Best of all, he wanted to get to know her. It seemed too good to be true, but if it was only a beautiful dream she didn't want to let it go before she'd explored all the possibilities.

Louise followed him through the overheated crowd to the hall, where more couples were draped around in various conditions and positions. She took her jacket off the hook near the door and slipped it over her shoulders, then left the flat without a qualm. There had been no point in trying to tell Gina or Ahmed where she'd gone. They were both in the throes of some more or less mind-blowing experience and wouldn't take in what she said anyway.

Outside it was chilly and Rick put a protective arm around her as he led her to his car, a shiny silver BMW. 'I got this with the proceeds from my movie star days,' he said ironically, seeing her admiring the vehicle. 'This and the flat are all I have to show for it, but I'm far happier with what I'm doing now.'

Inside the car Louise felt her tensions drain away and a delicious, drowsy relaxation fill her limbs. Rick's vibrant presence, accentuated by a hint of some sultry cologne, was making her feel something more than mere arousal. She felt sexy too, of course, more than she cared to focus on. But there was also a feeling of cosy familiarity, similar to how she'd felt with Martin in the heyday of their marriage. How was that possible, after knowing someone barely half an hour?

As the car sped through the dark, deserted streets Louise stopped puzzling and just enjoyed it. She knew she didn't have to put on an act with Rick, didn't have to make smart comments or try to impress him. They talked about ordinary, mundane things, like their favourite biscuits or kids' TV programmes. In no time at all they were drawing up outside a large house in Chelsea made of dark red brick, its white front door covered with brass furnishings. 'I have the garden flat, otherwise known as the basement!' he grinned, leading the way down a flight of stone steps.

The flat was not as spacious as Gina's but Louise felt very at home there. Rick opened some wine and put on some music. After they had chatted for a while he suddenly said, 'You look wonderful in that dress, Louise. D'you know what I wanted to do with you at the party?'

She shook her head, fiery cheeks compounding her embarrassment. He smiled, taking her hand. 'I just meant it would have been nice to dance with you, that's all. Can we do it now?'

Rick raised her to her feet and pulled her into his arms, where she floated dizzily around the room. The music was a slow ballad and Louise rested her head on his shoulder while her legs entwined with his and their hips swayed in unison, taking her into a realm of quiet contentment. She was aware of the powerful masculinity of his body, of the sex energy that was dammed up in him waiting to explode, but for the moment she was happy to rock gently in his arms and await developments.

When the music ended they stopped dancing and tender fingers tilted up her chin. Louise held her breath as his mouth descended, touching hers so gently at first that the hairs stood up on the back of her neck. His palms were smoothing over her shoulders, and her nipples were brushing lightly against his chest through the thin material. She looked up into the naked flame in his sapphire eyes and a great shudder of desire went through her.

He must have felt it too. Suddenly his mouth

was pressing more firmly, his tongue between her lips, and his embrace tightened, squashing her breasts against him. He reached down and felt through the open sides of her skirt to her stockinged thighs. Nimble fingers released her suspenders and the stocking-tops slipped down, giving him access to her naked flesh. He groaned faintly as his fingers smoothed a path up her inner thigh and found the silken pouch that covered her sex, already moist with her secretions. Louise longed for him to go further, but instead his hand came up to her breast and held it, his thumb rotating on her stiff nipple beneath the veil of chiffon.

'Louise!' he murmured, his lips still on hers. 'I'm so hungry for you, but I think I'll get indigestion if I eat you all at once!'

She giggled, slipped her hand beneath his loose shirt to feel the warm skin of his back. 'And I think I'm going to collapse if we carry on like this standing up!'

To her surprise he lifted her right off her feet and carried her into the bedroom where he laid her down on his bed. It was dark in there, but he lit a lamp then sat on the bed looking down at her. 'You're very special to me,' he whispered. 'Don't ask me why. I just know.'

'I feel the same way,' she smiled, gazing into his eyes where the golden lamplight was mirrored within the deep blue of his gaze.

Louise stretched out her legs languidly, enjoying the chance to rest them. Carefully he removed her shoes and then began to massage her toes through her stockings. She sighed and leaned back against the pillow, transported into bliss. His capable hands moved up her shins to where her stocking tops lay rumpled, and slowly pulled them down over her knees and finally over her feet until her legs were bare.

'Silky dress, silkier skin,' he murmured, his lips kissing her thighs with titillating softness. Louise felt all kinds of desires coming to birth in her. She longed to explore his body, to feel his firm buttocks beneath her palms and caress the sinewed strength of his thighs. She wanted to know what his secret dimensions were, the size and shape that men set such store by. But she held all those urges at bay, not wanting to spoil things by grabbing too much too soon. Instead she took her cue from him, letting him set the pace. He had started a slow-burning fire in her that would continue till dawn if he let it.

Lazily his hands lifted the black silk panels of her skirt to reveal the dangling suspenders. His hands went beneath her bottom and found the hooks that secured the garment. She lifted her pelvis and allowed him to undo it, discard it, opening up her pubic area to view.

The tiny triangle that held her pussy now held his gaze. For several seconds Rick looked down at the scrap of black silk before covering it with her skirt again. Louise felt a pang of disappointment. She moved her thighs and the silk rustled insistently, but his hands were no longer there. Instead they had travelled up to her neck, stroking it softly as his lips returned to hers.

This kiss was different, more sensual. For a few seconds she tasted the buttery tang of the Chardonnay on his lips then his tongue slid into her mouth in a delicious foretaste of what she hoped was to come. Lovingly Rick began to explore the inner recesses of her mouth with the tip of his tongue, and at the same time he was stroking her body with the silk of her dress, moving it around her stomach, breasts and thighs. Louise gave a voluptuous sigh. Her mouth was full of sweet saliva, mingling with his. She ran her hands down his long, muscled back and found the tight mounds of his buttocks which she stroked appreciatively.

His kiss deepened, growing more passionate as Louise clenched his behind and moved her pelvis up in a yearning bid to make contact with his body. His thighs moved over hers, pinning her down, and she felt the weight of him pressing hard against her. His tongue probed more deeply along the length of hers. She moved her lips against his, sensing the new urgency that had risen within him and which she could easily match.

Soon his mouth was travelling away from hers to the soft column of her neck, making her squirm with ticklish delight. Rick had his hands on both breasts now, kneading them, making the already hard nipples crave the touch of his fingers, his lips. Louise grew impatient with her dress, wanting him to tear it off her, but still the barrier remained between them. Then one hand found its way into the opening at her waist and lightly caressed her stomach beneath the silk and travelled up her midriff to brush against the lower slope of her right breast. Louise's whole body felt taut and strained, her breathing suspended as she willed him to carry on up and touch her rigid, aching nipple.

But his fingers travelled back down to her belly again and there they stayed while he bent his head and grazed the rosy tip of her breast with his teeth through the chiffon. She sighed and he mouthed it eagerly, although the feel of the wet stuff against his lips must have been strange. It clung to her breast where his saliva dampened it, stuck to the contour of her nipple.

'You're lovely in this dress,' he repeated. 'I can hardly bear to take it off you.'

'And I can hardly bear to keep it on!'

They laughed at each other, full-throated and free, their faces throwing radiance back and forth. Louise felt utterly happy, completely centred on her own pleasure. She turned over onto her stomach and let him unzip her, but then he spent ages just stroking her back through the opening and sweeping his hand over the smoothness of her rump. One finger slipped down between her buttocks, taking her pants with it. They stayed at the top of her thighs while he moved back up to pull down the straps of her dress.

Louise lifted her torso and felt the top half of her dress being pulled down over her breasts to her waist. It finally bunched around her hips while he pressed her down again and began to stroke her back once more. This time his fingers crept around to the side of her breasts, flattened beneath her. She moaned as the delicate skin responded to his feather-like strokes. The slow heat between her thighs was intensifying, sending out warm flurries of desire that confused her brain and befuddled her senses. I want him, she thought, like I've never wanted anyone before.

And the great thing was, he seemed to desire her just as strongly. As soon as she turned over onto her back Rick was at her feet and kissing his way up her legs until he reached her pubic mound. His kisses there, over the silk, were slow and reverent and she thrust her mons at him eagerly. But he went on to lick around the hollow of her navel, excruciatingly ticklish, then moved on upwards. Louise gave a long, grateful sigh as he at last reached her naked breasts and took first one, then the other nipple between his lips, rolling them gently and darting his tongue in and out. She felt his teeth graze them softly and she arched her back as the keenest of thrills passed through her. Her hands went to the top of his head where she ruffled his dark curls, and then she began tracing the delicate curves of his ears with her nails.

'This is heaven!' she breathed.

'Almost!' Rick replied, looking up at her from the comfortable cushion of her breast with a cheeky grin.

He continued his sensual mouthing of her breasts until Louise could bear it no longer. She wanted him naked, wanted to see the whole of his body at once, but she was too shy to mention it. The roughness of his sweatshirt was brushing against her stomach and his trousers felt coarse against her smooth legs. He had taken off his shoes, but his socks were still on his feet. Beneath his clothes she could sense that his body was muscle-packed but lean, the body of a man who knew how to look after himself.

'Please, Rick. . .' she begged, hoping he would know what she meant. He drew back, sat up and gazed at her. His brows were very straight and dark, a frame for the piercing blueness of his eyes beneath.

Now they were lifted quizzically. 'Louise?'

She sensed how much he liked saying her name. 'Can't we take our clothes off now?'

'You want me to?' With a swift, easy gesture he stripped off the shirt and revealed his top half. Louise feasted her eyes on the broad expanse of chest with just a smattering of dark hair in the deep ravine between his pectorals. She took in the solidly developed arms, and the lean abdomen that led down to a slim waist. His skin was lightly tanned, and it gleamed with health and vitality.

'Oh Rick!' Louise put out a tentative hand and laid her palm against his chest. She had never seen a man so beautiful in the flesh. He held out his arms to her and she pressed her face to the warm, flat pillow of his torso. It was like sheltering against a friendly rock.

He stroked her cheek protectively as Louise nestled in his arms, feeling archetypically female and submissive. Not that he was trying to dominate her. But set against all that impressive brawn she couldn't help feeling small and vulnerable. The emotions that were welling up inside her were unfamiliar, coming from some primal level of consciousness that she'd never plumbed before. They brought with them an overwhelming desire to be taken by this man, to be penetrated to the very core of her being.

'All right, you win,' he smiled, pulling the dress right off her until she only had her panties left half on. His hands roved freely and rapidly about her body, making every nerve-ending beneath her skin tingle fiercely. Louise lifted her mouth to him and he kissed her, drinking deep of her saliva, their tongues performing a loving dance. Then she felt his hands go to the rolled-down scrap of silk about her loins and finally uncover her sex, the soft-centred heart of her desire for him – and the focus of his desire for her.

Louise closed her eyes as he bent his head towards the junction of her outspread thighs. Gentle fingers parted her labia and she felt his warm breath on her opened vulva, a delicious prelude to the touch of his mouth. The tip of his tongue probed between her outer lips and found the deep chasm which was already filling with her juices. She moaned as he dipped into it, his hands slowly caressing her inner thighs, and a flood of pure joy went through her.

The lapping tongue moved upwards, found her distended clitoris and began to lick it hard, making Louise cry out in rapt approval. She could feel his hands stroking her behind, and then a finger found its way right round into her open sex and pushed straight in, as far as it could go. Her hips bucked in a reflex urge towards him as he delved deeper inside, his tongue still flicking rapidly across her throbbing nub. She squeezed on his finger and her arousal heightened.

Louise was very near to a climax now, and it wouldn't take much to push her over the edge. What it took, in fact, was for Rick to move one hand up to her straining breast and tweak her nipple. There was a flash of electricity that went both up to her ears and down to her toes simultaneously, then she felt the first shuddering spasms ripple through her lower regions, gathering force and breaking over her like a tidal wave. She spiralled through a series of wild convulsions that left her breathless, her pussy hot and pulsating, her chest heaving. Again and again she felt the powerful torrent of pleasure course through her. Then the ecstatic cycle began to subside and she sank into a state of profound relief.

When she returned to consciousness she was lying in Rick's arms. He was still wearing his trousers and socks, she noted with some amusement. Seeing that her eyes had opened he kissed her forehead then drew gently away. 'You're wonderful, Louise,' he whispered. 'But I have to be up early tomorrow, for a photo shoot – more's the pity. So I'll sleep in the spare room, not to disturb you.'

'It's all right. . .' she began, but he had already got up from the bed.

'Sleep well!' he smiled, switching off the light.

Louise was far too tired to argue. Alone in the darkness she tried to make sense of what had happened to her that night, but soon succumbed to sleep.

When she awoke in an unfamiliar bed, she quickly scanned through her memory of the night before and was overwhelmed by happiness. Rick, where was he? Then she remembered. He'd had to leave early. A blanket of disappointment threatened to engulf her so she got straight out of bed and opened the blinds. The décor of the room was classy but understated, a tasteful setting for the bed which she now realised was antique, with a marquetry design on the headboard. Probably a family heirloom or something. There was a door leading from the bedroom into an en suite bathroom.

After showering, Louise felt better. She got into her dress, feeling quite incongruously clad for daytime, then went out into the hall. A door opposite led into a small but well appointed kitchen and there was a note for her on the pine table: *Louise – that name will be just a kiss away from my lips all day! Please find your taxi fare on the dresser. Will phone tonight. Ricky xxx*

She put on the kettle and made herself some tea, feeling like an interloper. There was evidence of Rick everywhere: in the letter addressed to him on the mantelpiece, in the half-eaten pot of yoghurt in the fridge, in the green rubber boots by the back door. Somehow she hadn't thought of him as a gardener and yet, when she looked through the kitchen window, the garden was ablaze with flowers and tubs of herbs on a small patio.

Then she went into the sitting room and saw the current copy of *Arena* on the coffee table. She couldn't resist flicking through it but it took her two goes to discover the advert with Rick in. He looked so different with his hair swept back in dark waves, his eyes half closed against the bright sunlight, wearing an oatmeal linen suit and navy shirt. She smiled down at his face and vowed to buy her own copy forthwith.

Much as she would have liked to linger there, discovering more of Rick's personality through his surroundings, Louise knew she must get back or Gina would be worrying about her. She phoned for a taxi and reluctantly took the money on the dresser shelf since she'd left her cash at home. Then she pulled her jacket on, doing up the buttons to conceal her breasts. Conflicting feelings were making her want to get away, to reflect on what had happened without the subtle influence of being in Rick's flat to sway her mind.

The cab driver gave Louise only a cursory glance before whisking her off to Holland Park. When she opened the door to the flat mayhem met her eyes. As well as the usual post-party debris there were people sprawled all over the hall. She tiptoed through to her room and found a couple fast asleep in her bed. Feeling increasingly annoyed, and wishing she'd stayed longer at Rick's, she peeped in at the sitting room. The Chinese transvestites were piled in a promiscuous heap of satins, black wigs and naked limbs.

Frowning, Louise returned to her room and rescued a pair of jeans and a T-shirt, together with some underwear and shoes, then went into the bathroom which was mercifully empty. The only room in the flat that was, she supposed sourly. She dressed herself in more suitable clothes, picked up her shoulder bag from behind the door in her bedroom and hurried out as discreetly as she had entered.

For several hours she walked around the Sunday morning streets, buying a newspaper and trying to read it in the park. But her thoughts kept drifting back to Rick like homing pigeons. She knew that what they had shared last night could end up being a one-night stand, the aftermath of a party where everyone was prepared to let their hair down and lose their inhibitions. Don't kid yourself that he feels the same as you do this morning, she warned herself. But his note had promised that she would remain uppermost in his mind all day. Was he just a Don Juan, getting a perverse kick out of pretending to have 'romantic' feelings when he had no intention of seeing her again?

Although they'd talked almost non-stop – until the kissing had begun, of course! – Louise realised that she knew very little about him. She knew where he lived, but she could never bring herself to turn up there uninvited. Maybe Gina could tell her more about him.

But a strange reluctance overtook her when she thought about telling her sister. Louise had an urge to keep her experiences with Rick to herself, at least for the time being. She didn't know why, exactly, but she feared that Gina might ridicule her if she confessed to being in love with him. For that was definitely how it felt. Could she trust such extravagant emotions, when she was still married to another man. The thought was sobering.

Yet why should her heart care if she were divorced or not? Her love for Martin had died years ago and this new love had come upon her unawares. She hadn't been looking for a new relationship, not consciously anyway. And after all, Rick had made all the running, inviting her to his flat and then kissing her so sweetly and making love to her with such controlled passion. Whatever he had been seeking last night it was not a cheap thrill for himself. If she had tender feelings for him, she could be certain they were reciprocated. So went her reasoning process, on and on, round and round, until she tired of her own confused logic. Time would be the arbiter of both their feelings, she decided. She would just have to be patient.

Returning to the flat around noon she found most of the guests gone and Ahmed making toast for the four hangers-on who remained in the kitchen.

'Ah, Louise! There you are,' he smiled. 'Where did you get to?'

'I just popped out for a paper,' she said. It was only a white lie, but she felt her cheeks colour a little as she said it.

'How about some coffee? Toast?'

'No thanks, I had some earlier. Is Gina still asleep?'

'In bed, not asleep. Here, take this tray into her, will you? I reckon she deserves a rest this morning.'

Amidst a chorus of 'hear-hears' Louise went through to the main bedroom. Gina smiled when she entered and sat up, plumping up the pillows behind her shoulders. 'There you are! Ooh, breakfast in bed. Come and sit down and tell me how you enjoyed the party.'

'Very much,' Louise smiled, taking her seat beside the bed.

Gina's eyes had a red-rimmed look. Her dark hair hung in tousled strands to her bare shoulders where a couple of love-bites were visible, and there was a general air of lassitude about her. She drank from her coffee cup thirstily. 'The last time I saw you Rick was with you, then you both vanished. What did you get up to, you naughty girl?'

Louise thought quickly. 'Nothing much. We

went outside for some air and walked for a while. He's very nice, isn't he? When I came back I was really tired so I found a quiet corner and went to sleep.'

'Really?' Gina was frowning at her. 'That doesn't sound like much fun. Didn't you get off with anyone?'

'I had a few flirtations!'

'Is that all?' Gina sounded more than disappointed. As if Louise had let her down.

'I found it a bit much, to tell you the truth. I've never been to anything like that before. You could hardly expect me to join in with gay abandon – or straight abandon, come to that!'

Gina stared at her thoughtfully for a few seconds, then nodded. 'Mm, I suppose you're right. It was a bit of an experiment as far as you were concerned. Ahmed was afraid you mightn't be up to it just yet. But that means our party nights at the club are probably not a good idea for you either.'

Louise had hardly thought about her work at the club since meeting Rick. Right now she felt less than enthusiastic about it, but presumably she would change her mind come Monday night. 'I'm sorry. . .'

'Don't be, it's okay.' Gina reached out and clasped her hand. 'You've done really well so far, Lou. But now you know what company I keep maybe it would be best if you looked for somewhere else to live before too long.'

Louise nodded, feeling unaccountably miserable. Suddenly her whole life had come under scrutiny once more and she didn't much like what she saw. Last night had changed things, perhaps irrevocably, and she felt as if she were in limbo, unable to go forwards or backwards. She couldn't wait for Rick to phone that evening. Just to hear his voice would be a tremendous relief. Until she did she couldn't be sure of anything any more.

But then a dreadful thought struck her. What if he didn't phone that evening? Or didn't get in touch with her at all? What if she never saw him again in her life?

Chapter Nine

GINA WASN'T ALTOGETHER surprised when Louise decided to do no more than table dancing at the club for the time being. She knew that inviting her sister to that party had been a tactical mistake. Even so, she was a bit worried about her. Louise was acting strangely, spending a lot of time alone in her room when she was in the flat, going out at all hours and sometimes staying away all night. When Gina had tried to ask her about it she'd been rebuffed.

'If you're seeing a client behind Ahmed's back, watch out!' she told her grimly.

Louise had insisted, 'Oh no, it's nothing like that. I've just been spending nights in my old house, sorting things out.'

Gina didn't believe her for one minute, but she didn't press it. Relations between them were cool these days, and she didn't want to make the situation any worse. But when Louise told her she was moving out and gave a fashionable Chelsea address her curiosity was aroused once more. 'Surely you can't afford to live there on your own.

Are you sharing, or what?'

'Yes, but my flatmate won't be there very often. It's perfect for me right now.'

Her tone was still distant and Gina decided not to pry. But she might just call round there on the off-chance sometime.

Right now, however, she had other matters to occupy her. Ahmed had hired a new girl at the club and he was showing more than just a professional interest in her. Gina had to admit the girl was exceptionally good-looking. Her name was Yasmin and she was half Indian and half English, with pale coffee-coloured skin, long black lustrous hair and grey eyes. All the men were mad about her, and when she danced the snaky undulation of her slim hips, the suggestive thrustings of her pelvis and tight little bottom, and the controlled flexing of her pert rounded breasts awakened unexpectedly strong lesbian longings in Gina herself.

For a while she acted as house mother to the girl, who had never done anything but dance in discos before. She didn't need much tuition, having a natural talent and sex appeal, but she did need help in handling the men. Gina had never seen anyone get so much unwanted attention, so she kept an eye on the proceedings to make sure the girl wasn't pestered.

One night she saw Ahmed shepherding Yasmin out of the club just after midnight. Her shift wasn't supposed to end till two, so Gina went up to see what was wrong. 'Are you feeling ill, darling?'

Yasmin turned her beautiful, sooty-fringed eyes towards her and giggled. Gina recognised that look of schoolgirlish wickedness and turned a strange mixture of hot and cold inside. 'Ahmed, where are you taking her?' she asked softly.

'Home. We need to work on a few routines.' He patted the girl's rump affectionately. 'This young lady has ambitions, and I mean to see that she achieves them!'

Gina felt her heart racing as she struggled to maintain her cool. 'Good. Well, I'll be home in an hour or so. See you both then.'

It was a well-worn code, that she and Ahmed had used a dozen or more times. Sometimes, when they met a particularly sexy woman at the club or at a party, they would take her home with the idea of making love in a threesome. Usually the girl in question knew exactly what she was letting herself in for, and was fully acquiescent from the word go.

This time, though, her lover frowned back at her. 'I'd be grateful if you'd stay to lock up tonight, Gina. And when you return, please don't disturb me. I expect I'll be quite exhausted.'

Yasmin gave a knowing smile, stoking the fire of Gina's fury even more. Ahmed simply wasn't playing the game. He wanted this lovely creature all to himself, and was deliberately excluding her. Well, she wouldn't give in that easily!

Although she remained at the club for another hour, Gina could barely control her anger. It wasn't just that she felt cheated of a few hours of sensual pleasure, satisfying as that would undoubtedly have been, but she couldn't stand the thought of Ahmed having Yasmin all to himself, instead of sharing her. The idea that she could be simply jealous took some time to develop, but when she faced it Gina was quite shocked. She had lived for so long with the idea that she and Ahmed had an open relationship, free from the possessive pettiness that other couples displayed. But there was no mistaking the gnawing pain inside, compounded of her frustrated longing and a poisonous envy.

Unable to stand it any longer Gina finally handed the keys over to Karl, promising him a bonus for staying the extra hour, and took a taxi home. She entered the flat as silently as possible, removed her shoes and tiptoed through the hall, listening for any sound that might give her a clue as to their whereabouts. It didn't take long to work out that they had already graduated to the bedroom.

Softly Gina turned the handle of the door which Ahmed, in his arrogance, hadn't bothered to lock. She peeped through the crack and saw the couple on the bed, gilded with subdued light from the bedside lamp. It made a pretty scene. Ahmed had music playing too, soft and low, and a scented candle filled the air with jasmine as a tribute to the girl. All to put Yasmin in the mood, Gina thought sourly. Not that she looked like she needed it.

Hatred threatened to engulf her as she stood at the door, spying on the couple that she'd previously hoped to join. She knew there was no point trying to barge in on their love-making. There had been a steely look in Ahmed's eye that told her, unequivocally, 'I'm having this one all to myself.' Instead she drew some small satisfaction from the fact that, unknown to them, they were being watched.

Yasmin had stripped to her panties and Ahmed was completely nude. They were lying side by side, the girl fondling his erection while he played with her breasts, tweaking the dark brown nipples to hard points. Gina sensed that they hadn't got to the main action yet. They must have been taking their time. Maybe she'd been practising her lap dancing on him, or giving him a blow-job. As she gazed intently at the couple she felt a hot surge of lust hit her groin, taking her by surprise. She pressed her fingers to her delta over the thin skirt she was wearing and felt her clitoris throb when she located it.

Rubbing herself gently, Gina watched Ahmed remove the girl's white pants and reveal her luxuriant black pussy. His fingers dabbled for a moment or two in the crevice beneath, smearing the juices first over her pubic hair and then her gently rounded stomach before he moved back to stimulate her nipples. Yasmin gave a loud sigh and bent her mouth to his glans, moving round to push her pussy into his face. Gina couldn't see him actually licking but she could tell from the look on the girl's face that she was enjoying it very much indeed.

Ahmed was enjoying it too, if the size of his prick was anything to go by. It reared up and thrust itself into the round red 'O' of Yasmin's mouth. Her plump breasts were pointing downwards and soon his hands had grasped them, kneading them and drawing out the hard nipples while he sucked her off, making her lovely beige butt wiggle with twofold satisfaction.

Suddenly Gina realised that she was missing a trick here. Reluctant though she was to interrupt, however temporarily, her voyeuristic thrill, she left the doorway and hurried back on stockinged feet into the living-room. There she opened a drawer as quietly as she could and found what she was looking for. With a cunning smile on her face she returned to her vantage point at the bedroom door.

She lifted the black box to her eye and pressed a button. The shutter slid open, its slight click masked by the gentle notes of music issuing from the other black box beside the bed. Gina pressed again and there was a brief flash, but Ahmed and Yasmin were too preoccupied with each other to notice. He was thrusting his distended organ in and out of her open mouth at great speed, and she was bucking her hips in a frantic effort to match his accelerating libido. Suddenly she sat right back on his face with a loud cry as the white spray fountained from his glans over her breasts and stomach. It hung there in glutinous pearls as she orgasmed over and over, her stomach muscles rippling and her breasts shaking.

Gina felt her own insides quiver in sympathetic response to the other woman's pleasure but beneath her erotic excitement there was still that jealous anger. She took another couple of photos then retreated from the door. Going back into the living-room she paced around for a while, trying to control her mounting frustration. What she felt like doing was filling a bucket of icy water and thowing it over the pair of them, like a couple of randy dogs. Yet she knew that would only provoke Ahmed to the point of throwing her out of both the flat and the club. Sometimes it irked her that she was still so dependent on him. She had plenty in the bank, but nowhere else to go. What on earth would she do if her job at *Seventh Veil* came to an end?

When she'd calmed down a little Gina reflected that she had, after all, gained some vicarious satisfaction from spying on them. Her clitoris was still hot and throbbing, her nipples stiff and tingling, and she could feel how wet and ready her vagina was. Maybe if Ahmed bundled Yasmin off in a taxi soon she could reap the benefit of all that stimulation and have a monster session with her lover. If he had any strength left, of course.

It was time to find out. Gina returned to the bedroom door, still armed with the camera. She smiled to see that they were still at it, this time with Yasmin on top. The girl was rising and falling to the slow, voluptuous beat of the music, grinding her mons against his as she hit the root of his shaft, then remaining poised for a few seconds as she hovered above his cock, her pussy-lips caressing the sensitive glans. Ahmed was groaning as his roving hands alternated between her rotund buttocks and equally globular breasts.

Once more Gina struggled to quash the fervent desire to join them. She fantasised about sitting behind Yasmin as if they were riding the same horse, her labia spread against those warm, smooth buttocks and her clitoris rubbing between them. Her hands would be cupping those firm breasts from behind, playing with the adorable nipples, and her lips would graze on the delicate skin of her neck. Ahmed would find it extremely arousing of course, and would soon come. Silly man, why couldn't he see how good it would be for him if they were a threesome?

But perhaps he was breaking her in gradually, Gina thought, deciding to wait a while before suggesting such a bold venture. The idea that such delights might be hers in future made her feel much better, and the wild urgency of her desire returned in force. Now she envisaged herself with his prick inside her, sucking the sweet fruit of Yasmin's pussy as she rode Ahmed to her own delicious destination. She took some more photos then put the camera on the floor so she could ease the sudden upsurge of her sexual appetite.

Gina pulled up her skirt and put her hand down the front of her panties. Her pubic hair felt damp, and her clitoris bulged out so that her fingertips found it easily. She let out an involuntary gasp as the sharp sweetness of her arousal flooded through her, but neither of the others seemed to hear a thing. Through heavy lids she glimpsed them. Her lover had now decided to assert himself and had swivelled round to plunge into Yasmin from above, his penis and swinging balls clearly visible between his outspread thighs as he performed. Beneath him Yasmin thrashed and moaned her way towards a second shattering climax, her head turning this way and that on the pillow in her desperate quest for fulfilment.

The sight was too much for Gina's overloaded sensory system and she began to come in a flurry of hot spasms that had her moaning and swaying, one arm supporting herself against the door jamb. When the feverish orgasm subsided it was all she could do to pick up the camera and crawl on her hands and knees into the sitting room. She put the camera back in the drawer then flopped, exhausted, onto the sofa and was soon lost to the world.

Some time later Gina awoke to silence. She got up and switched off the lamp in the sitting room then looked at the clock: almost three a.m. Feeling she had a perfect right to make her presence known now she walked into the hall and found the main bedroom door wide open. The bed was empty, and Yasmin's clothes had been removed. A surge of cold anger swept through her. Had the pair gone off into the night together, to continue their dalliance undisturbed?

Gina stripped off her clothes and fell into bed, too tired to bother about what Ahmed was doing right then. The next morning, however, she was surprised to be awakened by voices. It didn't take her long to discover that Yasmin was still in the flat. Annoyed, she pulled on her robe and went into the kitchen only to find the pair of them laughing and joking over coffee.

'Good morning,' Gina said frostily.

Ahmed gave her a smile and a peck on the cheek, but his eyes still had that coldness in them that she'd detected last night. 'Morning, Gina. Hope you don't mind Yasmin staying.'

Gina poured herself some coffee from the pot then retreated to the corner. 'Not at all.'

But she did mind. And, increasingly, she had the idea that there was some hidden agenda. She finished her breakfast without saying much, then went to shower. When she came out of the bathroom, Yasmin was gone. Ahmed was still in the kitchen drinking coffee, a thoughtful look on his face. 'I'd like to talk to you, Gina,' he said.

She felt her heart plummet. Something in the tone of his voice told her that he had a plan in mind, one that he expected her to object to. He came straight to the point. 'I've offered Yasmin the spare room. She's gone to get her things then she'll be coming back this afternoon.'

'What?'

Gina could hardly believe he'd done that without consulting her. Okay, so it was technically Ahmed's flat, but didn't she have some rights as a sitting tenant, at least?

The look on her face made him continue, swiftly. 'She's been given notice to quit and she has nowhere else to go. It will probably only be for a few weeks. But while she's here I want you to be nice to her, okay?'

Gina's first reaction was outrage. But there was still an over-optimistic part of her that refused to be silenced. 'I see. You want a *ménage à trois* for a while, is that it?'

But if she'd had any hopes of sharing Yasmin with him they were quickly dashed by the stubborn look on his face. 'Technically, I suppose so. But I meant what I said last night, Gina. I'm keeping Yasmin all to myself. Do you have a problem with that?'

She struggled to control her feelings, pausing to light her first cigarette of the day. 'I'm not sure, I mean, where will you sleep? If you and Yasmin intend to take over our bed. . .'

'No, don't worry. We'll use the spare bedroom. I've no intention of humiliating you or anything, Gina. It's just that . . . well, Yasmin is rather special to me, that's all. It's a long time since I've wanted a woman so much.'

'I see.'

Gina drew nervously on her cigarette, her mind racing. 'In other words, I'm no longer the number-one wife. Is that it?'

'Gina. . .'

He put out his hand to her but she could see in his eyes that it was so. That awful, empty rage took her over inside and she felt sickened. 'What if I don't cooperate? I get kicked out, I suppose.'

'There's no need to react like that. After all, I was willing to let your sister stay here. . .'

'That was different!'

'Have it your own way. I've told you what will happen, and that's that.' He rose from his stool, wiping the toast crumbs away from his mouth with a serviette. For some reason the gesture provoked her uncontrollably. She picked up a mug containing coffee dregs and flung the brown mess over him, then walked out. Hot waves of adrenalin were flooding through her veins as she grabbed her coat from the peg in the hall and left, slamming the door behind her.

Gina walked round and round the park with long, rapid strides for about ten minutes before she began to calm down. Rational thought was still lacking, however. Three bloody years, she kept telling herself. That's what I've given him, and how does he repay me? Trading me in for a younger model. What a sad fucking cliché!

Slowly the desire for vengeance grew in her, and a plot began to hatch. It even made her smile. If she was going to lose her lover, her home and her job in one fell swoop then she might as well go out with a bang. It was her own stupid fault for tying up every aspect of her life with Ahmed. But there were other men out there, men who still found her attractive and desirable. She thought of David, with whom she'd had such a good time in Paris, and her mood lightened a little. But first she had some unfinished business to deal with. Walking with slow deliberation she turned back towards the Gothic-style house which now, looming through the dank mist of an autumn afternoon, looked to her more like a prison.

Louise stretched out in the luxurious bed and gave a long sigh of contentment. Rick had gone off early on a fashion shoot and she'd had a late night at the club, so it was good to be able to relax while the mellow autumn sun fell across the duvet in one big, golden swathe. She switched on the clock radio by the bed and some light, upbeat music filled the room. Today she would go to that Italian deli and buy the ingredients for a delicious pasta dish. She simply loved cooking for Rick. She loved doing anything for him. In fact, she simply loved Rick.

Although Louise still had her debt and divorce hanging over her she was at last on the road to recovery. Once her share of the mortgage arrears was paid she would stop working at *Seventh Veil* and find a more respectable job again. Rick had no idea what she did there. Or, if he did, he kept it to himself. She'd told him that she worked in an exclusive club, and he'd questioned her no further. Perhaps he'd rather not know.

She had also managed to conceal the fact that Gina was her sister. At some level Louise felt guilty about it, though she hadn't lied. When Rick had asked her to move in with him, after knowing her for less than a month, Louise knew that her life was about to take a totally new direction and she didn't want anything to spoil it. She'd already made one major break with the past and soon she would make another. Her destiny was linked with Rick's from now on.

Everything seemed perfect between Louise and her new lover. Their first dates had been wonderfully romantic – clubbing followed by midnight walks by the Thames, cinema visits followed by sexy suppers *à deux* – and always ended up with the most superb love-making. Now lying in bed, Louise was getting all hot and bothered just reminiscing. Her fingers trailed between her smooth thighs as she recalled their second session.

They had drunk quite a lot of wine that evening, and returned to Rick's flat eager to get their hands on each other. Louise started to tear the clothes off his back, but Rick gently stopped her and they'd taken things more slowly. When she was completely nude he ran her a frothy bath and washed her all over like a baby, arousing her gradually as he soaped her in all her intimate places. Then he had taken her through to the bedroom wrapped in a warm, soft towel and, very tenderly, unwrapped her like a birthday present.

Rick proceeded to consume her like a luscious fruit, his lips travelling all over her super-clean body and finally coming to rest between her thighs. His lips and tongue were expert in their caresses, knowing exactly how much pressure to apply and where, when to speed up and when to slow down, when to give all their attention to her pulsating clitoris and when to drink from the pool of her juices or dive deep into their source. After he had licked her to an exquisite climax she'd begged him to allow her to undress him, but he'd seemed strangely reluctant.

'What's the matter, Rick?' she asked him, ready to reassure him about his penis size if that was what was bothering him. It couldn't have mattered less to her.

As it turned out that was exactly what was bothering him, but not in the way Louise had expected. First he'd let her strip off his shirt to display his handsomely muscled torso once again. Then he'd undone his belt and fly and stepped out of his trousers. Her eyes had fallen automatically to the red Calvin Klein briefs and what she saw made her gasp. Beneath the cotton she could plainly detect the outline of a huge erection, far bigger than she'd anticipated.

He'd noted her surprise with a wry grin. 'Yes, I am rather . . . well endowed. It's a mixed blessing, though. Sometimes I think all women want me for is my big dick.'

'Is that why you didn't want me to see it straight away?'

He nodded, his blue eyes clouding a little. 'I was afraid the same might be true of you.'

Louise stared back at him incredulously. 'How on earth can you say that, after the way we've been together?' Her eyes had started to brim with tears. The thought that Rick might not trust their budding relationship as much as she did was too hurtful.

But he took her into his arms and kissed her forehead, smiling radiantly again. 'I was hoping you'd say something like that.'

'Silly!'

Louise tapped him playfully on the end of his nose and soon they were kissing again. This time she could feel his erection thrusting upward between their bodies, and her desire to become better acquainted with his penis grew to irresistible proportions. Slowly she slid down his body, her lips grazing his flat stomach, until she was squatting at his feet. Then she carefully lowered the pants over his mighty organ and took it between her palms.

It looked and felt like some exotic plant: a long, thick stem culminating in a pinkish-mauve bulb. Even the faint, delicious smell issuing from its glazed eye seemed vegetable rather than animal. Instinctively Louise leant forward and cradled it between her breasts. Rick closed his eyes and threw back his head with a moan as she bent her mouth and gave his glans an experimental lick. It was like sampling a hot ice-cream cone. She opened her lips wide until they encircled his helmet just above the ridge.

Although she managed to get about an inch of his shaft inside her mouth Louise found that stretched her to the limit. All her senses were on full alert as her tongue was flattened against the invading flesh. She could taste his bitter-sweet juices, smell his increasingly musky odours and feel the firm rigidity of his erection as it moved in and out off her lips at a cautious pace. Wondering how it would feel making similar progress into her pussy was an awe-inspiring thought, and a bit frightening. She was grateful to Rick for his gentle restraint and her desire for him intensified.

'Oh Louise, let me do something nice to you

too,' Rick pleaded, from far above her, his hands caressing her dark blonde hair.

They moved onto the bed and were soon embracing side by side, legs entwined and the thick staff of his penis pressing urgently against her belly. An overwhelming curiosity now seized her. Just what was it like to have such a huge member inside you? Already she imagined she could feel her vagina loosening and stretching to accommodate the giant penis, lubricating oils flowing free and making her vulva feel slick and welcoming. Rick's hands on her breasts were only increasing her hunger for him, filling her with cravings that only full penetration would satisfy.

Rick must have sensed her urgent longing because soon he produced a condom from beneath the pillow and began to roll it down his cock. Must be an extra large size, Louise thought as the latex stretched to its fullest extent, forming a second skin over the long shaft. He smiled up at her, his blue eyes sending her sweet signals of love and lust. 'It's probably best if you go on top,' he murmured. 'Then you can control the depth of thrust.'

Louise needed no encouragement to straddle him and place that shiny pink dome between her eager pussy-lips. She gasped as she felt the tip of it engage in her entrance but Rick made no move to push in further. He was letting her take the lead. She wriggled about for a bit, getting the feel of its warm strength against her soft and dewy vulva, taking the measure of it. She bore down on him experimentally and felt herself widen, opening up to him. Slowly she let herself rise and fall against his glans and each time it was a little easier to let him in. The best thing was the feel of his great shaft pressing against her clitoris as she moved.

'You have wonderful self-control,' she smiled down at him, her gaze lingering on the tanned and handsome contours of his face and chest.

'I've had to develop it. But with you it's harder than ever. You can't imagine how much I want to be inside you.'

'Oh yes I can!' she insisted with a smile.

The sensation of slowly easing him further in was exhilarating. Louise felt the soft tissues around her entrance stretch and give, allowing the huge shaft to slide in between her inner walls. She didn't have to contract her muscles to feel him. The massage that her G-spot was getting was fantastic, and already she could feel the blunt end of him nudging against her cervix. Louise kept the rest of his shaft at bay with her fingers while she slid gently up and down with sighs of bliss. It was heavenly.

Rick was getting off on it too, his breath coming in ragged bursts and his eyes glazed. She guessed it wouldn't take him long to come now and slowed down to make it last longer. He reached up and took her breasts into his hands, warming them. His thumbs began working her nipples up into hard, tingling studs and Louise knew that it would soon be her turn to reach that point of no return.

'Your pussy feels wonderful to my prick!' he grinned up at her.

The words almost triggered her right away, but she stopped moving and just waited a few seconds, relishing the feeling of being filled to maximum capacity. Every square inch of her internal skin was in glorious contact with firm, hot flesh and as she began to bear down on him once again the first shuddering hints of the pleasure to come rippled through her lower regions, making her gasp with renewed satisfaction.

'I think I'm about to come!' she murmured, squeezing his erect penis as hard as she could.

Instantly her orgasm strengthened, and the wild ripples that ran up and down the end of his shaft were enough to bring on his climax too. Making fierce animal noises, the pair of them wallowed in pure ecstasy together, firmly docked, and Louise began to feel as if something more than just a physical bonding was taking place. She seemed to be giving herself up to him, allowing their two consciousnesses to flow and merge until each knew what it was like to be inside the other.

When the spell faded, Louise lay snuggling up to his broad chest and knew that something wonderful had happened. A part of her was still fearful that it wouldn't last. After all, she'd known Rick such a short time. But she told herself that even if things didn't work out between them she wouldn't have missed the experience she'd just had for the world.

But things had gone from strength to strength since then. Louise sang gaily as she went about getting dressed and tidying up, looking forward to the meal she planned to cook before she left for the club that evening. She was so looking forward to the day when she would no longer have to work at *Seventh Veil*. Tired of saying no to the constant requests for lap dances and blow-jobs, she found it hard even whipping up the enthusiasm to perform a table dance these days. Fortunately she was no longer the 'new girl' since Yasmin had arrived. That took some of the heat off. The men were buzzing like flies around that honey pot, including, she'd been amused to notice, Ahmed. It was a good job Gina was not the jealous type.

Hard as it had been to tear herself away from Rick that evening, Louise arrived at the club on time. She was thinking about the brief session of love-making they'd managed to fit in when her lover returned from his photo shoot at seven, and her body was still hot and tingling with the after-effects. Maybe that would help her to dance better that evening. It was the sort of stimulus she needed these days.

After paying the taxi driver, Louise walked through the car park and into the back door of the building. She was about to enter the dressing-room when she noticed it was completely empty. That was odd: it should have been full of girls getting ready for the night's show. She went towards the swing doors that gave access to the main club room, and hesitated. There was a strange buzz of voices on the other side. None of this was normal, something was up. But what?

Warily she pushed the door and slipped through. A huddle of girls stood in the centre of the floor, some half dressed, staring at the walls with blank incomprehension or wide grins on their faces. Louise squinted at what they were looking at and gave a sudden gasp. All around the room were pinned poster-sized photographs of two people making love in various positions. At first she thought it was just some new idea for the décor – until she recognised the couple featured there: Ahmed and Yasmin!

Mystified, she rushed up to ask Janice, 'What's all this about?'

She shrugged. 'No one knows for sure. It was like this when we arrived. We don't know who put them there, or if it's meant as a joke or what.'

'If you ask me, it's no joke,' Sarah put in. 'I reckon someone wants to embarrass the pair of them. And I've a good idea who that might be!'

'What do you mean?' Louise asked, nagging doubts forming at the back of her mind.

'Look, if they've been put up maliciously we'd better start taking them down,' Janice said. 'Ahmed won't be pleased when he arrives. And neither, I should imagine, will Yasmin.'

'Too late!' Sarah muttered.

All eyes turned towards the swing doors, through which the man in question had just entered, closely followed by Gina.

Chapter Ten

GINA'S HEART WAS thudding loudly in her ears as she followed Ahmed in through the swing doors. She saw the other girls surveying her handiwork and her pulse rate speeded up even more, this time with annoyance. She hadn't counted on there being an audience for her little photo show. If only Ahmed had arrived at the club earlier!

But now everyone knew about his affair with Yasmin, evidence of which was blazoned over the walls in all its blatant glory. Not that anyone would care – except for the parties concerned, of course. She saw her lover turn ashen, his eyes contracted into steely points as he swung round and faced her. 'Is this your doing?' he snapped.

'What if it is? Don't you think it livens the place up a bit?'

Ahmed's hand flipped out at speed and caught Gina across the cheek. Her eyes smarted as the spot began to burn and she put her hand up to cover it. But worse than the physical pain was the disgrace. She had a brief glimpse of Louise's stricken face as she turned away. Ahmed had never struck her before.

'Bastard!' she muttered, making for the swing doors.

Behind her she heard him call out, 'Tear them all down, girls! I don't want to see a single scrap left on those walls when I come back into this room.'

Gina broke into a trot, desperate to get away from him, but as she reached the dressing-room door rough hands pushed her through and slammed the door behind them. Ahmed caught her wrist and twisted it painfully, making her cry out.

'What's the meaning of this?' he snapped. 'How dare you make a laughing-stock of me and poor Yasmin in front of the other girls!'

Fear had Gina gripped by the throat so she could hardly speak. She stared wildly at him, realising how far down the path of jealousy she had gone. But why? For three years she had accepted that he was free to screw whoever he chose, as indeed she was herself. Why had everything changed with Yasmin?

The same question seemed to be surfacing in Ahmed's mind as he stared into her face, searching for clues to her uncharacteristic behaviour.

'What the hell do you think you're doing, Gina?' he asked her, quietly now but in a more menacing tone. 'You're acting like a jealous cat. What's going on?'

She shook her head, near to tears. 'I don't know, really I don't. It's not like me, I know. But when you brought that girl back to the flat something seemed to snap in me.'

Ahmed's expression was still cold, but he had

loosened his grip on her. 'You spied on us and took photos. That I suppose I can understand. But to put them into the public domain, that is completely out of order. I'm only glad that Yasmin hasn't seen them, poor girl.'

'Where is she?'

'She wasn't feeling too good this evening so I told her to stay at home.'

Gina felt relieved. It was Ahmed she'd wanted to get at, not Yasmin. Even so she would probably get to hear of it. Suddenly she felt horribly ashamed of what she'd done. A sense of unreality took hold, as if she'd been in some altered state and suddenly returned to normal.

Then she remembered that Yasmin was going to be staying with them, indefinitely. Her old anger returned in a flash. 'I can't put up with her living with us for much longer,' she said.

Ahmed's eyes darkened again. 'In that case, you'll just have to move out.'

'*Me* move out?'

'Yes, you. I've promised Yasmin she can stay, and there's nowhere else for her to go. She's young and vulnerable, Gina. You can look after yourself.'

'I don't believe I'm hearing this! Three years I've been living with you, and now you're throwing me out without a qualm.'

'No, you can stay. As long as you are nice to Yasmin. Those are my conditions.'

'While you fuck her under my nose, is that it?'

'It's never bothered you before.'

Their argument was becoming circular. Again the weird sense of unreality had returned, together with the scary prospect that Gina could ruin her entire life in one fell swoop if she wasn't careful. She endeavoured to pull herself together. 'If I were to move out, you'd still let me work here at the club, wouldn't you?'

He gave her a strained smile. 'As long as you behaved yourself. The question in my mind now is how do we undo what's been done this evening. I think we need some kind of damage limitation exercise, don't you?'

Gina felt a sense of foreboding. She knew that look on Ahmed's face meant something. But what? She began to get out of her clothes and into her working togs. But Ahmed was still turning things over in his mind. When she had changed Gina lit a cigarette and sat opposite him, trying to appear unconcerned, but her pulse was racing.

'I know,' he said suddenly, his eyes brightening. 'Since your crime was public, your punishment shall be also. I shall see that you are thoroughly disciplined on Thursday night.'

Gina shuddered. Thursday night was Fetish and CP night. Up to now Gina had always been the one to administer chastisement, not receive it. She was well known as a dominatrix, and the clients queued up to be thrashed by her own fair hand. Ahmed could not possibly have devised a more humiliating punishment. Or, she grudgingly admitted, a more fitting one.

It was hard getting through the rest of the evening. The other girls were wary of being seen talking to her and she felt shunned by everyone, including Louise. Not that her sister had been over-friendly of late. Gina had found out, through the club grapevine, that her sister was living with Rick Morley and was angry that Louise hadn't told her directly. After all, she knew both of them. But when she'd tackled her about it all she'd got were pursed lips and shrugged shoulders.

Despite the frosty atmosphere in the club that night, Gina went through the motions with her regular clients but when the time came to go home she felt relieved. As she and Ahmed rode in silence through the streets of the capital, she couldn't help wondering how much longer she would be calling the Kensington flat 'home'.

During the next few days Ahmed did his best to keep her and Yasmin apart. Not that Gina had any desire to talk to the girl, but it was painfully obvious that he would not let the pair of them be alone for a minute. What was also plain, although less obvious, was that Gina had been subtly demoted from her position as his chief consort. Now it was Yasmin who joined him in the master bedroom while Gina had to make do with the spare bed. Yasmin also shared candlelit suppers with him, while she had to make do with a tray in what was now her room. Gina's charge card at her favourite department store was terminated, while Yasmin went on extravagant shopping sprees. Without having to say a word, Ahmed was making it clear that the process of degradation had already begun.

By Thursday night Gina was secretly in a state of trepidation. She tried her best to hide it, not wanting Ahmed to think that she feared him. But inside she was shaking. As she was getting ready to go to the club Ahmed entered the spare room where half her costumes were now stored in the small wardrobe. He went through them quickly, selecting what he wanted her to wear.

'I think this white silk and lace bra with the matching G-string,' he said, casually tossing them at her. Inwardly, Gina shuddered. The outfit offered no protection whatsoever to her buttocks, being little more than a thong around her waist and between her buttocks. Over it he wanted her to wear a black silk mini-dress with white apron and cap.

'The French maid's outfit?' she said, frowning. 'Isn't that just a bit too traditional for your taste, Ahmed?'

He merely smiled pleasantly at her, adding a frilly white suspender belt, sheer black stockings and black high-heeled shoes to the pile on the bed. Dutifully Gina put them on. No doubt he was planning some kind of playlet to entertain their clients. They wouldn't need a script. The ritual used a form of words that they had perfected over the years and each would take their cue from the other.

The Seventh Veil was packed that night and Gina had the uneasy suspicion that Ahmed had been spreading the word about her public penance. She knew the evening would be a test of her nerve and she was steeling herself to remain cool and in control. She couldn't see Yasmin but all the regular fetish girls were there, each distinguished by her costume. The submissives wore dog collars and chains, some with rings through their nipples; the rubber addicts sweated in latex catsuits; the bondage girls, some hooded, were confined in leather outfits with buckles and straps. It was a bizarre scene but, to Gina, a familiar one.

Less familiar was the skimpy costume she was

wearing herself. Normally she wore full dominatrix gear such as her tight-laced black rubber corset, Madonna-style bra with holes for her lipsticked nipples to point through, studded leather G-string and leggings or zippered lederhosen and, of course, her most vicious-heeled shoes. Her make-up would accentuate the image with black or scarlet lips and she would always ensure that her hair was elaborately styled, supplementing it with hairpieces where necessary.

Tonight, though, the tiny skirt and minuscule G-string left her feeling uncomfortably open and vulnerable. Her hair was drawn back in a simple French plait under the white cap and she was showing only a little cleavage in the square-necked dress. Ahmed nodded his approval as she mingled with the crowd, a tray of party canapés around her neck. The clients murmured compliments too, often in a knowing tone, and Gina was aware that the tension was mounting all around. The cabaret was due to start at eleven, and around that time everyone made sure they had a drink and a seat at one of the tables, preferably with a companion who shared their particular passion by their side.

As usual Ahmed took the stage to introduce the proceedings. He looked immaculate in his dinner jacket and Gina felt a faint stirring of the old attraction he'd had for her as she waited in a state of mixed trepidation and excitement for her cue. The first entertainment featured the 'pony girls' who trotted obediently around the small stage, tossing their long blonde manes before a riding mistress who flicked their rumps with her whip and made them go through their paces. They were followed by a masturbatory episode of foot fetishism, and then a performance by 'Nudini', self-styled 'Bondage Queen', whose act managed to combine escapology and strip-tease as she struggled out of a coiled mass of ropes and chains.

Gina knew her moment was coming when Ahmed took the stage again and help up his hand for silence. He put on his best MC manner and breathed into the microphone. 'Good evening, ladies and gentlemen. Tonight we have, as the climax of our show, something very special. As most of you know, for quite some time our premier pussy-cat here at the club has been the lovely Mistress Georgina. Take a bow, Mistress!'

He waved in her direction. Embarrassed, Gina rose from her seat and gave a mocking curtsey, which everyone applauded. Then Ahmed resumed his spiel. 'Well, from time to time Georgina has committed a few little peccadilloes. After all, she's not perfect. Who is? But I have to say that just recently our little pussy-cat used up her ninth life. Yes, she did. Which means that tonight she is going to have a little taste of her own medicine.'

The men started to whoop and cheer, causing Gina's heart to flip anxiously. It was all she could do to appear unconcerned. She picked up one of the titbits from the tray she had placed on the table and popped it into her mouth. It was like chewing on chalk.

'Georgina, would you come up here on stage please?'

She rose slowly, deliberately, smiling back at

the grinning faces all around as if the act had been well rehearsed and she knew exactly what was in store for her. Her progress towards the platform was laden with sexual emphasis as she swayed her hips and wiggled her bum. Ahmed held out his hand and pulled her up the two steps until she stood beside him, hands on hips, surveying the crowd with a knowing grin.

'Tonight, gentlemen, you will have a rare treat!' Ahmed promised, smiling suavely. 'You will see the Mistress of Correction well and truly corrected. Note that she is not wearing her usual costume, but one far more suited to her new submissive role.'

The men whooped again, and some of the girls had the temerity to cheer. Gina scowled at them, and Ahmed wagged his finger. 'Naughty, naughty! Now I want you to kneel before me, Gerorgie, and show how willing you are to subject yourself to discipline.'

Gritting her teeth, Gina did as she was told. The carpet had been removed and the wooden platform was hard under her knees. She was afraid of snagging her tights but she stayed there, head bowed, until he bade her rise again. Behind her she could hear someone moving furniture about. When she got to her feet she saw that the whipping frame had been brought on by two of the girls, and she began to tremble. Always, in the past, she had been the one to administer the whip or the cane but never before had she been subjected to the same treatment.

Strong hands seized her and led her over to the frame where she would be secured. The two girls wore only leather harnesses and tiny G-strings.

They stripped off her maid's uniform until she was in her underwear, then strapped her wrists and ankles to the frame. The bra was a half-cup and her breasts spilled out of it, allowing her rosy erect nipples to peep through the steel bars. Then they pushed the button which made the frame slowly revolve, turning round so that she was facing the audience and then presenting them with her almost naked *derrière*. The men cheered loudly, keyed up for the spectacle.

A fleeting thought went through Gina's mind as she rotated in suspense: thank God Louise isn't here! It was a relief that Yasmin was nowhere to be seen either. As long as her humiliation took place only in front of clients and fetish girls it wouldn't seem so bad. She waited patiently for Ahmed to finish addressing the audience and produce his whip or cane.

'If you're going to be pussy-whipped,' he was saying, 'then there is only one appropriate instrument: the cat o'nine tails!'

One of the girls brought the instrument to him on a red velvet cushion. He took it and brandished it, the nine thongs rearing from the stout leather handle like vicious snakes. When Gina glimpsed it she shuddered at the prospect of those cruel lashes biting into her defenceless flesh. The frame made one more revolution and there, stepping onto the stage, she caught sight of a figure that made her gasp. The girl wore a shiny black leather collar, gauntlets, a tight-laced corset, and leggings all studded and linked with silver chains. Her shoes were black patent, also laced and with very high heels. Although the girl's identity was concealed beneath a frilly black rubber mask, Gina knew in an instant who she was.

So this was to be Ahmed's final humiliation of her! The significance of choosing Yasmin to administer the whipping was not lost on Gina. He was spelling out, in no uncertain terms, what she had feared: that her heyday as his lover and partner was over, and a new star was about to take centre stage.

Yasmin walked towards him slowly, her hips swaying seductively. The wave of applause reached its height then died away, to be replaced by hushed expectancy. Gina caught a glimpse of her tormentress as she swung round on her heel, whip in hand, and began to walk towards the frame with her bright red lips curved into a smile. Gina felt herself breaking out into a sweat. Her pulse was racing and her mouth was dry, but there was nothing she could do about it. All she could hope for was that, when the time came, she would not lose her nerve.

The strains of 'Hard-Hearted Woman' could be heard as Yasmin took up her position on the small podium, from where she could easily lash out at the naked buttocks spread out on the metal bars. For a couple of revolutions Gina was in suspense, her wrists and ankles already beginning to chafe. But then she heard a cheer as the new dominatrix raised the black leather handle and prepared to strike. No sooner was her behind within reach than Yasmin struck. There was a staggered crack as all nine lashes hit the air and then the stinging points landed on her naked behind like pepper shot. Gina flinched involuntarily, clenching her buttocks against the pain.

As the crowd came into view again Gina could see the men staring at her lasciviously, taking in every second of her agony. She stopped focusing on them and gazed sightlessly into the crowd, willing her eyes not to let her down by watering. As the torture-scaffold continued to rotate, Gina braced herself for the second bout of lashes, tightening her buttocks and holding her breath so that when the blows rained down on her poor cheeks again she would not cry out.

To her relief the impact of the second strike was less severe since several of the thongs missed their target, the smarting only lasting for a few seconds before a dull hot ache took its place. Gina's glazed eyes skimmed the crowd and then it was time to steady herself for the third assault. This time the thongs caught her equally on both buttocks and she could feel every individual impact. Despite her self-control she winced, and the crowd caught sight of it as she came into view. Catcalls and whistles followed, only making her all the more determined to maintain her steely demeanour throughout the session.

'Three down, three to go!' she heard Ahmed say. 'I must say our pussy-cat is standing up well to her sentence. And Madame Yasmin is wielding her power superbly! Let us have a round of applause for the beautiful new star amongst our galaxy of glamorous *grandes dames*!'

When she heard those words Gina felt despair seize her. He was as good as announcing to all and sundry that Yasmin was taking over from her, that she was being demoted. She struggled to keep a check on her anger, telling herself that now was not the time to show how upset she was. The whipping frame turned again, the bright spotlight exposing her body in every detail to the scrutiny of the audience. She could not afford to give anything away. Her face was set in a controlled mask, her muscles tense and her breathing shallow. Three more strokes: how could she stand it?

By a supreme effort of will she managed to endure unflinching to the end, even though Ahmed urged Yasmin to thrash harder and, at the final turn, she obeyed, the rawhide searing into Gina's behind like branding irons. But with it came immense relief, the knowledge that she had survived and, in some small measure, that she had achieved a victory over Ahmed. If he had expected her to break down in tears, or cry out in pain, he had been disappointed.

The two girls came on to undo her bonds and a spontaneous round of applause broke out, which Gina acknowledged with a bow and a wry smile. She then turned to Yasmin, whose glittering eyes were just visible behind the mask, and gave her a sneering grin before hurrying from the stage and straight through the swing doors into the dressing-room. There, finding herself alone at last, she burst into tears.

After a few minutes she pulled herself together and lit a cigarette. She found some cold cream and smoothed it into her throbbing buttocks, wincing as her fingertips touched the inflamed flesh. Her whole being was in turmoil, but one thing she was sure of: she couldn't go back to the flat tonight. It would be too degrading. What Ahmed and Yasmin had done to her that evening had robbed her of every vestige of self-respect.

She picked up her bag and began to look for her purse to see if she had enough cash for a hotel room.

Then she saw her small leather address book and had a better idea. She flicked through until she found Louise's phone number. That girl owed her one. At least one. Staggering off to the pay phone, Gina felt her heart lighten a little. She put in her coin and dialled the number. There was a long wait but eventually someone came to the phone.

'Hi, Rick. This is Gina!' she said, trying to sound as normal as possible even though it was past midnight.

'Gina? What do you want? We were just going to bed.'

He sounded suspicious. She tried to placate him. 'I'm sorry. I wouldn't normally have rung you so late but I'm at the club and I need a place to stay tonight. Just for tonight.'

'Well I don't know what Louise will say. . .'

'Just ask her then, would you? Please?'

There was some conversation that Gina couldn't make out, then Louise came to the phone. 'Gina, what's the matter? Is anything wrong?'

She sounded so sweet and concerned that Gina felt the tears well up again, but she stifled them and said, 'I've had a bit of a rough time and I need somewhere to go tonight. Can I stay with you, please?'

'Of course. But can't you tell me what's wrong?'

'Later, maybe. I'll get a taxi, be with you in under an hour. See you!'

By the time she got to the flat Gina was feeling a lot better. Her behind was merely sore, instead of agonisingly tender, but more importantly her spirit had been soothed too. Rick had already gone to bed when Gina arrived. He had an early morning shoot, but Louise also hinted that he'd left the pair of them alone to have a chat. For that, at least, she was grateful.

'It's good of you to put me up like this,' she began, sinking gingerly into the soft leather sofa. 'I just couldn't face going back to the flat tonight.'

'Well, you put me up when I had nowhere to go, so I'm only returning the favour,' Louise said coolly. 'What happened tonight? Were you at the club?'

'Yes. Ahmed decided to punish me for what I did the other night.'

'What, putting up those photos, you mean? I thought you were really stupid to do that.'

'I know. I suppose I wasn't thinking straight. Anyway, he's had his revenge good and proper now.'

'What do you mean?'

'I think he's trying to get rid of me and put Yasmin in my place. I suppose I should have seen it coming. After all, I've had three years. That's a pretty good innings, don't you think?'

Louise frowned, her hazel eyes looking genuinely concerned. 'You mean he's kicked you out of the flat?'

'And the rest! I was wondering if I could stay here for a couple of nights.'

'I see.'

Louise was still frowning, sunk in thought, and Gina reckoned she could guess exactly what was going through her mind. 'It's okay, I'm not planning to move in with you and Rick. I just need breathing space, that's all.'

'It's not that. It's just . . . well, he doesn't know you're my sister.'

'Ashamed of me, huh?'

'Not of you, no. But I want to stop working at the club. I've had enough of all that. I want to start over again.'

'And I don't fit with the new image, is that it?' Gina found a cigarette in her bag and lit it, inhaling deeply. 'Well, don't you worry your pretty head about me. Soon as I can find somewhere else to live I'll go. It's not as if I haven't got money in the bank.'

'I'm sorry, Gina. You look like you've had a hard night. Do you want a drink?'

Gina gratefully accepted a brandy. She didn't want to talk about her ordeal at the club that evening. It didn't seem necessary. Especially if Louise wasn't going to be there any more.

'Have you told Ahmed you're leaving?' she asked her.

'Not yet. Rick is going to try and get me some modelling work.'

'Hah!' Gina smirked at her sister through the haze of smoke she'd just blown out. 'Only modelling you're likely to get through that man is topless, or worse. Wise up, Louise. Don't let men rule your life. Get back in control.'

Louise stiffened. 'You don't know what you're talking about. Rick and I really care about each other.'

'Don't kid yourself, girl. The only thing you care about is his big dick.'

'What would you know about it?' Louise flared, her eyes green points of anger. 'I knew you'd be like this. That's why I didn't want to tell you at first. You're so damned cynical, Gina. But this time you're wrong. It's more than just physical between us. We love each other.'

'Oh, that little four-letter word again! I suppose Martin was just a flash in the pan and this is the real thing. Isn't that how it goes?'

Louise made a visible effort at self-control. 'Look, you're obviously in no mood for a proper chat and I'm tired. Bed's made up in the spare room. I'll see you in the morning. Night.'

Gina waved her glass at her and put her stockinged feet up on the sofa. She leaned her head back against a cushion and closed her eyes. The sounds of water running in the bathroom lasted for around a minute then she heard Louise entering the bedroom. To fuck Rick the Dick. Gina giggled, the brandy taking effect. She wondered if there were any of the old videos about, the ones she and Rick had made together. That would definitely give Louise something to think about!

Chapter Eleven

'I'M GIVING IN my notice at the club tonight,' Louise announced. Gina looked at her sister's determined face and sighed. When would the silly bitch ever learn? Even if she couldn't learn from her own mistakes, she now had her sister's example to go by.

They were washing up the breakfast things. The flat was quiet and the kitchen was filled with a mellow light that filtered down from the street. It seemed idyllic, but as she dried a china plate with a tea-cloth Gina felt some elder-sister responsibility to introduce a note of caution. 'Are you sure you're doing the right thing? I mean, you still owe money on the house, don't you? And you've only just moved in with this guy. Talk about on the rebound!'

Louise gave a starry-eyed smile. 'Rick says he'll take care of everything. I only owe about three thousand on the mortgage now. He says I can consider it a loan. Once the modelling assignments start coming in I'll be earning that much a month. Imagine, Gina!'

'Yeah! Imagining is about as near as you'll get. Look, sweetheart, you're forgetting one thing. Rick the Dick made his money out of hard porn films. He's got the equipment, as you're no doubt well aware by now. Do you really want to end up making sleazy movies?'

'Rick's put all that behind him now. The modelling he does is all very respectable. I've seen his photos. They're in *Arena, Vogue, Harpers & Queen.* I'm not saying I'll get such prestigious work. Not at the beginning, anyway. But he's going to introduce me to his agent on Monday morning, and. . .'

Gina held up a weary hand. 'Spare me the details, darling! Let's just say I'll believe it when I see it. But in my opinion you're a fool to trust a man with a track record like that after only knowing him a couple of weeks.'

Louise turned away, tight-lipped, and began stacking the plates in a wall cupboard. After a while she turned and said, 'Well what are you going to do, anyway? If Ahmed asks after you tonight, what shall I tell him?'

'Tell him I'll be back at work on Monday. I just needed a breather. He'll understand.'

'And what about somewhere to live?'

'I'm going flat-hunting straight away. Any shopping you need?'

Louise frowned. 'No thanks, I'll get my own. Look, I don't mind you being here, Gina. But I wish you wouldn't poke your nose into my business, okay?'

'Okay. I'll get my bag and be on my way then.'

The flat-hunting went better than Gina had expected. She found a couple of rooms quite near the club. The district wasn't too savoury but the flat itself was very pleasant, so she put down a deposit and arranged to move in on Monday. Already she'd decided that she would continue working for Ahmed, even though they would no longer be lovers. It might even work better if theirs was a purely business relationship. After all, it was the clients who mattered most at *Seventh Veil*, not the internal politics of the staff.

She wasn't worried that he would turn her down, either. For all his faults, Ahmed was a fair-minded man and he would consider that Thursday night's little spectacle had more than compensated for her earlier misdemeanour. Gina smiled as she thought of how she could turn her new place into a love-nest for her regulars. The landlord probably wouldn't find out, and if he did then she could afford to give him a sweetener on top of the rent. Ten years in the business had taught her how to handle these things.

Rather than get in the way back at Rick's place, Gina decided to eat out that night. She returned to Chelsea around eleven, entered the flat with the spare key Louise had given her, and found Rick there alone in front of the television, a bottle of wine at his elbow.

'Hi, Louise gone to work?' she smiled breezily, hoping to pre-empt any trouble.

He threw her a suspicious glance. 'Yes. She was wondering where you'd got to, as a matter of fact.'

'I thought it best to leave you two love-birds alone, so I ate out.' She flopped down into an armchair and kicked off her shoes. 'Mind if I have a glass of your wine?'

He rose and fetched another glass from the cabinet, pouring her a generous measure. She took it and smiled sweetly up at him. 'Quite like old times this, isn't it, Rick? Remember when we used to drink that Spanish plonk to keep our spirits up? Or, in your case, your pecker. I thought alcohol was supposed to have the opposite effect, but with you it always worked a treat. Cheers!'

His blue eyes cooled as they looked at her. 'All water under the bridge now, Gina.'

'So I gather. Little sister has been telling me you've gone legit, as they say.'

'*Sister?*' He started out of his chair, a deep furrow between his brows.

Gina laughed. 'You mean she's not told you yet? Ashamed of me, probably. She has no idea how far back you and I go. Or how far we went, come to that!'

'Sisters?' he repeated, bewildered. 'You mean to say you two are related?'

She sipped her wine. 'Half-sisters, actually. Same mother, different fathers. We lost touch when I left home at sixteen, but she came looking for me when she was in trouble. Now it's my turn. Well, that's what families are for, isn't it?'

'I can't believe this. You're so utterly different.'

'In appearance, maybe. But we're the same under the skin. We both have our mother's flighty temperament.'

'That's incredible. But now you mention it, I can see some resemblance. Something about the eyes. And your figures are not dissimilar.'

'Well, you'd know all about that, wouldn't you? Tell me, Rick, is she a good lay, my sister?'

'God, Gina, you're disgusting!'

'It's a reasonable enough question. When she first came to live with us Louise was practically a virgin. She'd been married for three years, but she was still naive and inexperienced. Ahmed had to break her in so she could perform at the club. You do know that's what she does, don't you?'

Rick gave her a disgusted look. 'You haven't changed, have you, Gina? If there's a chance to spread some poison, you'll take it. And in answer to your question, yes I do know what work she does. She hasn't told me in so many words, but I know the scene and I put two and two together. Anyway, it doesn't matter now because she won't be doing it any more after tonight. If I can put all that behind me, so can she.'

Gina drained her glass. The wine seemed to go straight to her head, making her woozy. Being with Rick was reminding her of old times. Times she had once wanted to forget, but which now had a certain rosy glow about them. After all, it had been fun for a while, hadn't it? *Wild About Willy* – wasn't that the name of the one they'd won the porn Oscar for? She held out her glass for more wine and Rick divided the remains of the bottle between them.

'Don't you ever think of the old days, Ricky?' she asked him with a smile.

He gave a reluctant grin. 'Sometimes.'

'Me too. All those dreadful films we churned out. At the time I never bothered to keep the free copies. Now I wish I had. After all, they showed me at my most youthful and sexy.'

'You're not looking so bad now.'

She smiled at the unexpected compliment, and a flicker of the old Rick showed in his blue eyes. Encouraged, she asked, 'I don't suppose you've got our masterpiece, have you? It would be great to see it again.'

'As a matter of fact I have.'

He stood up and walked over to a cupboard. Gina's eyes followed his neat behind across the room. In the loose tracksuit he was wearing she could see the outline of his buttocks, tight and firm as ever. Something fired inside her, setting her libido on slow burn. She watched him take two videos out and hold them up, showing her the covers.

'Oh, *Wild About Willy* – you have got it!'

He grinned. 'That was the crowning glory of both our careers, wasn't it? No plot, hardly any dialogue, but plenty of action.'

'Remember that tacky awards ceremony, where the MC got completely pissed and dropped the Oscar? Whatever became of the golden dildo, by the way? Don't tell me you've got that too!'

'No, Old Shorty got that. Used it as a doorstop, or so he said.'

'Shorty Klein! Now there's a name I haven't heard for years. Whatever became of him?'

'Last I heard he was publishing a fetish mag. Shall I put this thing on, or what?'

'Oh, yes please!' Gina giggled, settling on the rug in front of the television with her back to the sofa. Rick put the video in the slot and pressed the remote, then came back to sit on the sofa just behind her. She leaned back, wanting some physical contact, and her shoulder brushed his thigh. Tacky music filled the room and then the credits came up, making her giggle as she recalled the rest of the cast.

While the video progressed, showing her arrival at the 'Mr Muscle' contest where Rick was supposed to be the main contender, Gina felt her old warm feeling towards him reviving. He had been the favourite of her male leads, always professional in his approach and never failing to deliver the goods. They'd had lots of laughs, too. Now, as they watched the fruits of their efforts, the giggles returned in force.

'Oh God, do you remember the problems we had with my nipples in that scene?'

'You mean when Shorty wanted them flaccid?'

'Yes! I was supposed to play the innocent, and he wanted to show my nipples slowly getting aroused as I watched you going through your poses. Trouble was, it was so damn cold!'

'I seem to remember someone's hair dryer being called into service!'

'The lengths we went to!' Gina giggled at the unconscious innuendo. 'Well, the lengths *you* went to, anyway! You never had any trouble performing on cue, did you? Fast forward to the locker-room scene, Rick. I want to see you in action!'

They watched in silence as Rick emerged from the shower with just a towel around his waist and found Gina there, wanting his autograph. The camera zoomed in on the enormous bulge below the white towel, then cut to show Gina's eyes opening wide with sexual curiosity and her tongue flicking across her red lips. It was strange seeing it all again, after so long. As the towel was slowly drawn aside and the full extent of his erection was revealed, Gina felt an unmistakable twinge of desire and her pussy began to feel wet and open. She shifted position so that she could clench her thighs and ease the sudden throbbing of her clitoris.

The atmosphere in the room had subtly changed from one of jokey reminiscence to erotic tension. Gina didn't need to wonder whether Rick was feeling as aroused as she was. Over the time they'd worked together they had developed a kind of sixth sense that allowed them to tune into each other's feelings. She was amazed to find it still there. Even without looking at him she could sense the electric charge around him, knew that his massive hardness on screen was matched in real life, and an even more urgent pang of lust struck her, deep within.

Watching herself now on screen as she took his stiff member between her hands and knelt to kiss the rearing glans, Gina knew that what had made their acting special had been the spark of genuine attraction between them. She kept her eyes fixed on the television, fearing the consequences if she turned to look at Rick. The scene progressed to full-blown fellatio. Gina smiled to recall how she had trained to be able to take as much of that thick shaft into her mouth as possible. Practising first on a rolling pin, she had then asked Rick is she could rehearse with the real thing, which had led to a very satisfying session at her flat one Sunday afternoon. Was he remembering it too?

'You were always the best at sucking cock, Gina.'

His voice, thick with desire, startled her and she turned round to see Rick looking down at her, his eyes smouldering with the kind of lust you couldn't fake. She was seized by an overwhelming longing to see that prodigious prick once more, and it seemed to coincide with his equally compelling urge to show it to her. His hand was at his fly, unzipping it as his other hand reached out for her. At the touch of his fingers on the nape of her neck Gina shuddered, her whole body responding eagerly to this first green light.

At the back of her mind was a warning red light, but it was faint and easily ignored. Now fantasy and reality were merging indistinguishably as the action in the room mimicked that on screen. Almost without thinking, Gina found herself kneeling between Rick's open thighs, her lips and tongue exploring the well-remembered contours and musky taste of that wonderful organ. So familiar was the situation that Gina could almost hear the whirring of the camera, was half expecting to hear Shorty's voice call out, 'Cut! That's perfect, folks! Another red-hot blow-job in the can!'

Rick's hands reached down and pulled her shirt out of her waistband, making her shiver with anticipation. Still working her tongue around his glans, she feverishly undid the buttons and shrugged out of the sleeves. Then she unhooked her bra, levering the straps down over her arms until her breasts were completely bare. He gave a groan and seized them with both hands, squeezing the ample flesh and making Gina moan in response. The video proceeded unobserved as they gravitated onto the floor, where they soon managed to strip each other of the rest of their clothing.

Lying on the rug, Gina spread her thighs wide for Rick to perform cunnilingus on her. 'You were always the best at this, too,' she told him throatily, as his tongue unerringly found her clitoris and began to give her the kind of stimulation she most appreciated. She could feel the wild surges her libido was making as the years melted away and once again they were Rick the Dick and Queen Gina, undisputed superstars of the porn movie world. When his tongue began to probe her sex and she felt herself on the verge of coming, Gina also felt a renewed pride in her own achievement. It was no wonder that she'd been the best in her day. She'd never had to fake an orgasm in her life.

It had been a quiet night at the club for once, and Louise was thankful for it. Knowing that she had to face Ahmed after hours and tell him she was quitting had put a dampener on her performances. So when only three requests for a table dance came, and she spent more time than usual dancing on stage, the loss of income was more than compensated for by her relief that she didn't have to go through the motions.

She also had more time to observe what was going on around her. With Gina absent it was obvious that Ahmed was grooming Yasmin to be a star performer. He was introducing her to some of the wealthier clients and she was putting on a sexy act for all of them, wiggling her tight butt and thrusting out her small but well-shaped boobs. Soon she would be progressing beyond lap dancing and into the private stuff, no doubt ending up entertaining selected clients at Ahmed's flat. In every way she was taking over from Gina, so how long would her sister stand for being out-ranked?

Not long, she suspected. But with her looks and experience Gina was well able to look after herself. Maybe she would set up on her own as a dominatrix, or find work in another exclusive West End club. Well, she was welcome to it. Although Louise had found the world of exotic dancing an exciting alternative to office work, the glamour had begun to pall and now she couldn't wait to give it up. Especially now she had Rick. Whatever else she felt about her sister, Louise would always be grateful to her for throwing that party!

By the time she came off stage at the end of the night, Louise was dreaming of a new future with the man of her dreams. She must have had a special glow about her because Ahmed stopped her in the corridor with a grin. 'You're looking pleased with yourself,' he commented.

'Oh Ahmed, I wanted a private word with you, please.'

'Okay, step into the office. I'll be with you shortly.'

While she waited Louise felt nervous. She couldn't help thinking of Gina's reaction when she'd told her she was stopping work. Was she in for another lecture, this time from Ahmed? Well, it was none of their business, she told herself defiantly. They knew nothing of the love between her and Rick. She trusted her lover implicitly, and she wouldn't let her optimism be dampened by anyone, least of all anyone who had an axe to grind.

But when Ahmed appeared and she blurted out that she wanted to give in her notice, he said, 'Well I'm not surprised. You're not really cut out for this work, are you, Louise? I could tell from the start. Once you'd got over the novelty value it became hard work. And then when you stopped doing lap dances I knew it wouldn't be long before you gave it up altogether.'

'You don't mind, then?'

He shrugged. 'No one's indispensable.'

Including Gina, she thought wryly. With a bright smile she said, 'That's all right then. How much notice do I have to give?'

'As a matter of fact I interviewed a new girl only yesterday. She's very keen but I told her I had no vacancies at present. If she's still available, she can have your job and you needn't come back. I'll phone you tomorrow.'

A wave of pure relief swept over her. She hadn't realised how much she was dreading having to carry on at the club. Ahmed was right, she'd never been cut out for it, not really.

As she rose to leave, he said with a smile, 'You and Gina are like chalk and cheese, aren't you? But you'll both do okay, in your different ways. The one thing you've got in common is guts. Good luck!'

Louise felt quite fond of him as she shook his hand. But something told her their paths were unlikely to cross in future.

As her taxi sped back across London, Louise was looking forward to being with Rick again. Hopefully Gina would have gone to bed, but she knew Rick would wait up for her. He always did, even when he had an early call. They'd probably sip some wine together, then start kissing and cuddling on the sofa until the urge to make love became too strong. Then they would hurry to get ready for bed, to share the passion she'd been looking forward to all day.

On weekends it was different. They often stayed in bed for hours on end, surfacing only to grab some fast food and keep up their energy for love-making. Louise hoped her sister had found a flat of her own by now. With any luck she'd be moving out tomorrow, leaving the place to her and Rick again. Not that she begrudged Gina a bed for the night. It was just that her cynical attitude to love was beginning to get her down.

Louise could hear the TV playing as she entered. It sounded like a steamy late-night movie. Good, that would have got Rick into the mood. Not that he needed any incentive! She took off her jacket and put down her bag then opened the sitting room door. Rick was nowhere to be seen, but over the back of the sofa she could just see the television screen. Forget mere 'steamy' – this movie was positively pornographic!

She stared at the image on the screen. A dark-haired naked woman was kneeling with her back to the viewer, her tongue snaking up the shaft of an enormous penis. It's as big as Rick's, Louise thought. The actress moved in between his thighs and took the organ between her breasts. The camera moved in too, giving a shot of the man's cock cradled in her cleavage, then it panned up his tanned, muscular torso and came to rest on his face for a few seconds. Although his eyes were closed in an expression of rapt concentration, Louise recognised him at once. But what was Rick doing, running his old porn videos?

Both fascinated and repelled, Louise stared at

the screen where the woman now had her head bent right over Rick's penis and was licking it enthusiastically while she rubbed her breasts up and down the shaft. Suddenly she looked up and winked at the camera. A shock ricocheted through Louise's body as she recognised her sister's face.

So this was what they used to do together! No wonder Gina had taken a sceptical attitude when it came to Rick settling down in a steady relationship. She'd known him in the days when he'd been prepared to have sex with anyone, and probably not just in front of the camera. But he had finished with the past and was starting a new life. Louise was confident that she would be a major part of that life too, wouldn't she?

Suddenly she realised that the moaning sounds she could hear were not coming from the screen. Louise stepped forward and rounded the end of the sofa, then stopped in her tracks with a horrified gasp. There, sprawled on the rug, were the naked bodies of Rick and Gina in the sixty-nine position, their enthusiasm for the task rivalling that of their screen performances as they licked and sucked each other towards a climax.

'No!' Louise yelled, seizing the first thing that she could find and throwing it at the pair. The cushion bounced harmlessly off Rick's rump but served its purpose of alerting them to her presence. Rick scrambled hastily to his feet, his handsome face a study in tortured consternation, while Gina continued to lie there on the rug with a sneering smile on her face. Right then, Louise didn't know which one of them she hated more.

'You bitch! You bastard!' she yelled, turning to

run from the room. All she knew was that she wanted to get away from that hateful scene of double betrayal.

But she didn't make it to the door. Rick's strong arms caught her in their embrace and, although she kicked and struggled wildly, held her firmly until she had calmed down.

'Louise, please forgive me!' he pleaded. 'We got carried away watching our old video. It doesn't mean a thing, honestly!'

'It means I can't trust you, either of you!' she snapped.

'Look, if we'd intended to deceive you would we have done it right here on the floor when you were due to return any minute?'

Louise was stunned for a few seconds, but she soon recovered. 'The fact is you *were* doing it. And if I hadn't come in right then. . .'

'Then the chances are that we'd have come to our senses and stopped. Honestly, Lou, it's the truth. We've both been drinking, and. . .'

'Ha, good old alcohol! The time-honoured excuse for behaving like a bastard. So you were both drunk. Well that's all right then, we'll forget all about it. Hope you don't have too bad a head in the morning!'

Seizing her chance, Louise stalked from the room and hurried into the bedroom. She shut and locked the door, wanting no more to do with either of them that night. Sobbing bitterly into the pillow, she ignored the urgent rapping at the door and, when everything at last went quiet, took off her clothes and crept beneath the duvet, feeling wretched. Confusion reigned inside her head as she replayed the images of her sister and her lover, images that merged with those of the video to make a vivid, true-life scenario that tormented her. Gina had warned her that love with Rick wouldn't last, but then she had been the very one to ruin it. Just what was going on? Had her sister acted out of jealousy?

It was hard to come to any other conclusion, but whatever Gina's motives Louise couldn't excuse Rick. He was the one who had hurt her most. She knew what her sister was like, knew how jealous of Yasmin she'd become and how she'd tried to take revenge on Ahmed. It was even possible to understand how she'd become the woman she was, given the kind of life she'd led since she left home. But Rick had seemed different. She'd taken his declarations and promises deeply to heart, believing him to be a reformed character. What an idiot she'd been!

Although her tears had subsided they had left an ache in her heart, and an emptiness in her soul. It was all over betwen her and Rick. She would have to move out, and she would still have her debt but no means of paying it off. Her divorce was coming up soon – how ironic! Her prospects, that had seemed so bright just a short while ago, had suddenly been reduced to nil. Wearily Louise turned on the pillow, *his* pillow, she reminded herself bitterly. She'd sold almost all her possessions in a futile attempt to make a small dent in her debt. Now she had nothing left to lose but her pride, and some good that would do her!

Eventually Louise drifted into a fitful sleep. In the morning she woke with a dull sense of foreboding and then remembered everything, triggering more tears. After an hour or so of self-pity she made it to the bathroom and splashed her red, puffy eyes with cold water then went into the kitchen, desperate for a black coffee. Today she would have to sort her life out, find somewhere to stay, see if Ahmed would take her back just for a few weeks until she found another job. The way she felt now she'd be prepared to do anything for the clients just to get enough money for a deposit on a flat.

When Gina came into the kitchen wearing her black silk robe Louise picked up her coffee mug and sprang to her feet, intending to leave. But her sister gave her a rueful smile.

'Wait, Lou. I think you and I should have a little chat, don't you?'

'Like hell I do! What makes you so sure I want to talk to you?'

'Because you're in an almighty mess and you've no one else to turn to, that's why. Now just listen for a few minutes, will you? I'm not used to apologising or explaining, so don't give me a hard time, okay?'

Louise sat down again and slumped over her coffee. She wouldn't look at Gina while she was talking but stared sulkily at the pine table top. One night Rick had made love to her on that table, while she was preparing a meal for him. She angrily quashed the memory and began to listen, despite herself, to what her sister had to say.

'What Rick told you last night wasn't quite true,' Gina began hesitantly. 'We didn't just get carried away, and we weren't all that drunk. At least, I wasn't. I made a deliberate play for Rick, led him on. It was me who asked him to put the video on in the first place, and once I saw that he was getting turned on I took advantage of him.'

'Why? To get at me?'

Louise met Gina's eyes. They looked sad and world-weary. Was it possible she could be genuinely sorry for what she'd done? Well, it was too late now.

'Actually I thought I'd be teaching you a lesson. I see now that was stupid of me. I wanted to show you that any man could give in to temptation, be unfaithful. Especially one who had lived the kind of lifestyle that Rick had. But I've been thinking about it since. . .'

'When, last night, while you were in bed with him, you mean?' Louise regretted her bitter outburst when she saw the look on her sister's face.

'I spent the night on the couch. Anyway, I realised that what you and Rick had was something I've never had, and I suppose I was jealous. It's not just physical between you and him, is it? When you threw that cushion at him and he looked up, I saw how stricken he was, how terrified that he'd ruined the one thing that really mattered to him. And I felt terrible too. I felt about the same as when I broke Mum's vase.'

'What?'

'Oh, you don't remember, I suppose. But it was why I finally left home. She had this precious vase, some kind of antique. We were having a screaming match and I broke it. The look on her face horrified me. I felt she wished I'd never been born, she hated me for coming into the world and spoiling her life. And I couldn't stand that feeling, so I just got up and left. The one thing in my life I regret is that I never went back to tell her I was sorry.'

There was silence. Louise stared at her sister, tears starting in her eyes. She rose slowly and went to give her a hug. The hurt inside her was still there, but for the moment it seemed less acute.

'Anyway,' Gina smiled up at her through tear-washed eyes. 'At least I can say I'm sorry to you. And I really mean it.'

Chapter Twelve

TRY AS SHE might, Louise couldn't forgive Rick for what he'd done. What Gina had said about men was proving horribly true. She'd been through the drink and debt scene with Martin, now she was going through the infidelity scene with Rick. Presumably next time came the violence. It was enough to put you off sex altogether. Maybe she should try women.

The trouble was she ached for him still, like an addict suffering withdrawal. Gina had gone to her new flat leaving the pair of them alone, but there was an atmosphere you could cut with a knife. Louise mostly kept out of his way and when their paths did cross she met every overture of his with a stony stare or, if absolutely necessary, a curt reply.

Ahmed rang to tell her that the other girl had taken her job and would be starting on Monday. Louise hadn't had the nerve to plead with him to take her back. Instead she went off on Monday morning to the Job Centre, pretending that she'd come straight from her old job at Newbolt's. The little matter of her P45 could be sorted out later.

When a temporary job at an estate agent's came in she jumped at it. Maybe they'd help her find a flat, too. She couldn't bear living with Rick any longer than was necessary.

Then he had to go away on a three-day shoot. Although part of her was relieved, once he'd gone Louise missed him terribly. Despite the fact that they'd hardly been speaking lately she had still grown used to seeing Rick about the place, and she still derived a sneaky pleasure from looking at his great body. Unbeknown to him she'd been through all his portfolios, drooling over the sexy images. If only the inner man had matched up to the outer one, she'd told herself with a sigh. Still, you couldn't have everything. Obviously Rick was a good bet for a one-night stand, but she'd made the fatal mistake of falling in love with him. End of story.

The job in the estate agent's was boring as hell, but at least it was only for two weeks. Louise found it hard adjusting at first. She kept wondering what her colleagues would say if they knew about her not-so-distant past. Then it occurred to her that the same was probably true of Rick. When he posed for those suave *Vogue* and *Arena* shots, did the ghost of Rick the Dick ever rear its ugly head? The thought seemed to bring her closer to him. Not that it made any difference. He was still out of bounds to her, both physically and emotionally.

That evening there was nothing to interest her on the TV so she began browsing through his video collection. Inevitably, after all the *Die Hards* and the *Rockys* she came across his own porn videos. They had names like *Good and Hard* and *Rocks Off!* and if they weren't in plain wrappers the covers bore pictures of impossibly pneumatic women and muscle-bound men. She flipped through them idly.

Then she found one with such an alluring picture of Rick on the front that she was instantly seduced. He was wearing nothing but jeans with the zipper half down, and his thumbs were in his belt. He had a gorgeous tan and his chest and hair were wet, as if he'd just been in the sea. Behind him was a beach scene, with Baywatch-style babes gazing adoringly at him. Louise slotted it into the player and pressed the remote. The same picture came up on the screen along with the title: *Adonis on Paradise Beach*.

Louise settled back on the rug and let the video run. She was soon mesmerised by the images of Rick bathing nude in a rock pool, being chased by nubile mermaids all over the beach and then dragged protesting into a cave where they each had their wicked way with him. As she watched the girls performing acts of fellatio on him, rubbing themselves with his penis and allowing him to tongue their pussies, Louise could feel herself becoming unbearably hot and randy. It was days since she and Rick had made love, and in the intervening period she'd felt too miserable to think of pleasuring herself. But now her libido had returned with a vengeance and she could hardly wait to satisfy it.

While the video presented her with yet more tantalising pictures of Rick *in flagrante delicto*, Louise started to pull off her tights. She could feel the dampness at her crotch and knew that she was already horny as hell. Just because she was through with men didn't mean she'd stopped being a sexual being, she reminded herself ruefully. Time for a spot of totally safe sex, without risk of disease, complications or heartbreak!

Her nipples were practically bursting through the cups of her bra by the time she pulled the lacy trimming down and got to them. She groaned with relief as she felt the hot little buds between her fingertips, but soon the throbbing in her crotch became equally unbearable and she put one hand down the front of her pants to feel the hard nub at the top of her pussy.

Through bleary eyes she gazed at the TV screen, where Rick was sucking the full breasts of some buxom redhead while he stroked her furry bush. Louise thought she knew exactly how the woman felt. The memories of all her nights with him returned to torment her, making her arousal seem more painful than pleasurable. Helplessly she called his name out loud, over and over, trying to ease the aching void within her soul as well as the fevered needs of her body. If only he were there with her now, in the flesh, not just a flickering image on the screen!

Then, somewhere in the back of her mind, she registered the familiar click of the front door as a key turned in the lock. Her hand froze, and her heart seemed to suspend its pulsing beat as she listened hard, intent on ascertaining whether her ears had played her false or not. Was it just wishful thinking that had conjured up the sound of someone entering the flat? A shiver ran down her spine as she heard the door open and close. There was a heavy tread and then the door of the room was opened.

'Louise? Are you still up?'

It *was* Rick! What was he doing back so soon? One thing was obvious: he couldn't see her from the door because she was on the floor in front of the sofa. The irony of it almost made her burst out laughing. Hastily she pulled up her jeans and pulled down her top, clicked the remote to obliterate the video and put her head up above the sofa. 'My God, you scared me! I thought you were an intruder.'

'I'm sorry. I tried to phone but it was either engaged or off the hook.'

Louise went to check. It hadn't been put back on its cradle properly. That was her fault. She'd called Gina earlier in the evening when she was feeling lonely, but there had been no reply. When she turned back to Rick she was blushing guiltily, not because of the trouble with the phone but for what she'd been doing when he came in. Her crotch still felt overheated and tingly. She made an effort to appear normal. 'What happened to the photo session?'

'The camea crew were in a road accident. Nothing too serious, but two of the lads had to stay in hospital for observation so Joe cancelled the shoot.'

'I see.'

Louise felt ridiculously awkward. The semi-silence of the past few days had been broken, but she still didn't know what to say to him. Her embarrassment deepened as he noticed the empty video case on the floor by the TV. A slow grin brightened up his face, making him look irresistibly boyish. 'So! No need to ask what you've been up to while I was away!'

He picked up the box, looking quizzically at the picture on the front. 'Adonis, huh? What happened to that guy? Wasn't he torn to pieces by jealous women or something?'

Louise trawled her memory. 'Killed by a wild boar, I think.'

'Oh. Well if I had the choice of being massacred by a gang of women who hated me, or killed by one single woman who loved me, I know which I'd prefer.'

His impossibly blue eyes were searching hers now, holding them with their dazzling radiance. Louise felt herself melt in the smouldering heat of his gaze, that was searing its way into her soul, purging her of all her fear and despair until only a deep, desperate longing for their previous closeness remained.

Rick came to sit on the floor beside her, his long legs in front of him. He sighed and stretched. It had been a stressful day for him. Louise fought the urge to offer him something to eat or drink, as she'd once have done. Instead she took the video out of the machine and replaced it first in its box, then in the cupboard. 'Well, I think I'll go to bed now then.'

She turned to the door but he leapt to his feet. 'Louise! Please don't go yet. I want to talk.'

Although she had stopped in her tracks her body was tense all over. She said nothing but just stood there in turmoil, like a potential suicide on the ledge. 'Talk' sounded so innocuous, but in her present state it could lead to other things, things she wasn't sure she wanted. Then she felt the firm touch of his hands on her shoulders and her heart sank. If he made any more moves towards her she was lost.

Gently he turned her round to face him. Louise tried to avoid his eyes but it was impossible. They drew hers irresistibly, with the blinding light of their candour.

'What happened between me and Gina was a stupid mistake. It was wrong of me. But it meant absolutely nothing. I want you to know that.'

'It might have meant nothing to you. To me it meant that I could never trust you.'

'I know, and I'm terribly sorry. If I could turn the clock back I would. But it was just. . .' He sighed, struggling to express himself. 'It was like a kind of reflex, you know? She wanted me to put that video on, and then it was so easy to slip back into the old ways.'

'But that's just the point. How could I be sure you wouldn't slip back into those "old ways" again?'

Rick led her to the sofa and they sat down side by side, but Louise couldn't relax. She sat there primly, as if she was being interviewed. Yet all the time her body was crying out for him in silent agony, wanting so desperately to be in his arms instead of an arm's length away.

'I don't know,' he admitted miserably. 'All I know is I've lost the most precious thing in my life through being stupid and careless. I had dreams for us, Lou. And now they're all shattered. And I'm shattered too.'

She knew how he felt, but a stubborn voice kept insisting that it was all his fault. He was the one who had spoilt it all, not her. Yet Gina was to blame too. Not just for seducing him, but also for putting doubts in her sister's mind. Louise asked herself if she would have reacted quite as strongly if those doubts and fears hadn't already been there.

'I don't know what to say,' she sighed. He reached out and took her hand. A flood of warmth went through her, breaking down her reserve. 'I feel sh . . . shattered too.'

Helplessly she let the tears flow and let herself be taken into his embrace where she gave full vent to her feelings. She soon realised that she was crying for complex reasons. Not just for herself, but for Rick and Gina too. They'd all, in their different ways, sold out on love. Gina had come to believe she would never have it; Rick believed that he'd had it and lost it; Louise knew that what once was sweet could so easily turn sour.

With the heat of his body enveloping her, Louise slowly felt her heart begin to melt. She hugged him close, wanting him so much, and the fears began to recede. His lips found the soft skin of her neck and deposited tiny kisses there that made her spine tingle. Deep inside she felt herself opening up to him again. It was a fragile truce, but it was a start.

Rick's mouth moved up and onto hers, parting her lips with his tongue until they were in full contact, their mouths engaged in lush and sensual kissing. The last dregs of Louise's bitter defensiveness leached away, leaving her willingly vulnerable to his advances. She clung to him in passionate abandon, letting his hands stroke her wherever they wanted, and soon she wanted to caress him too. She undid a button and slipped her hand through his shirt to find the smooth, honed flesh beneath.

'Oh Lou, I love you. Really I do!' His lips breathed into her ear, then returned to hers, letting her bask in the glow of his love. Their kiss deepened, and then she felt his lips slide from hers to graze on pastures new.

Nudging its way beneath her top, his mouth travelled up to the warm divide between her breasts and made her groan with delight as his tongue probed down the sensitive cleft. She could feel her breasts straining against the bra cups, and put her hands behind her back to unhook the garment. Rick's lips moved to her nipples and a fountain of pure pleasure seemed to spurt up inside her, making her pussy feel liquid. The need inside her was compelling, and to her amazement she suddenly heard herself say, 'Please, Rick, kiss my pussy for me!'

Obediently he stripped off her jeans and panties, his eyes gleaming with anticipation as he stared briefly at her naked mons. She opened her legs for him and saw his gaze take on a new dimension of joy and wonder. But then, as he bent his head to do her bidding, Louise realised that something wonderful had indeed happened. She had asked a man to pleasure her, told him exactly what she wanted doing, and he had obeyed without question.

It was the first time this had happened to her. With Martin she had never dreamed of asking, only passively accepted what he did to her. Even while she was working at the club and revelling in the new sense of power it gave her, she had not known this unique satisfaction. Rick wanted to please her, wanted her to be happy, simply because he loved her. The knowledge came as a revelation.

'Rick, would you stroke me with your fingers there too?' she asked, experimenting with her new-found licence.

His tongue continued to flick across her clitoris while his finger played around her entrance, teasing her by entering a little way and then retreating, making her more and more hot for him. He put two fingers into her, then three. She thought about his penis entering her and shuddered hungrily. But perhaps it would be good to wait a while. Her pussy was wet and fully open, but she wanted to explore his body before she went any further.

Eagerly she swivelled round into the sixy-nine position, felt for the hard, thick erection and took it between her palms. It increased even more as she began to caress it with soft, sensitive fingers, revelling in its solid dimensions and the velvety texture of the skin.

'It's all yours to play with,' she heard Rick say huskily. Louise bent her head to lick across the domed tip. It leapt in her hands like a wild creature and she felt an answering flutter in her core that made her want him all the more. This time she didn't want to be on top. She wanted Rick to possess her utterly, to fill her with a surfeit of flesh so that she was utterly satiated, complete. Oh, how she ached for him!

Tenderly Louise held the rampant organ between her breasts, relishing the way it thrust into her cleavage, her lips and tongue tasting the salty sweetness that was beginning to issue from his glans. Rick was still paying homage to her pussy, preparing her with his lips, tongue and fingertips, gently stretching and softening the delicate tissues of her vagina to accommodate the length and girth of his organ. Soon she felt wide open, her slick entrance able to take his bunched fingers easily. She moaned out her desire and he groped for the condom in the pocket of his discarded jeans, then positioned himself to enter her.

With a deep sigh, Louise felt his glans slip between her labia and enter her. She pushed against him, hungry to feel him inside her, but he held back so that she wouldn't have too much of him too soon. Slowly he eased himself into her, triggering the most exquisite sensations as her desire for the most intimate embrace of all was gradually realised. Her vaginal walls caressed the thick shaft as it progressed further and further in and she could feel herself yielding to him, letting him penetrate her more deeply until his glans was lodged right up against her cervix and every inch of her was satisfyingly filled.

Rick began to move back and forth, sliding his shaft against her inner surfaces with infinite gentleness and giving her clitoris a good rubbing in the process. She sighed and leant back, her breasts thrusting upward, and soon felt his soft lips against her yearning nipples. His tongue savoured them, sucking and licking, until they swelled and firmed up even harder than before. The pulsating currents whirled from her breasts down to her stomach and on to link up with her clitoris, turning her body into one escalating circuit of desire that felt like it would overload if she didn't climax soon.

'Oh, Louise!' Rick moaned as his own relentless drive gathered pace.

Louise could feel the heat of him enveloping her like a tropical noon, and his raw, sexy aroma reached her nostrils, fuelling her arousal. She tightened her thighs to feel the thick root of his shaft moving back and forth, his balls slapping rhythmically, and she cried out in ecstasy at the sudden onset of her orgasm. Again and again her vagina seized his penis in a fierce embrace until she was aware of Rick shuddering and gasping, joining her in an ecstatic consummation that was utterly fulfilling.

For a while afterwards he lay in her, like a great ship docked in harbour, and Louise derived a bittersweet pleasure from their closeness. She'd got what she wanted: one last act of love with Rick. Whatever happened she would never regret it. But as the minutes ticked silently away and the afterglow faded, all the old insecurities started to return.

It was on this very rug, Louise reminded herself, that he and Gina had been making love just a couple of nights before. Well, he was a great lay, she had to give him that. But that was all he was, all he could ever be to her. She'd been foolish to imagine that their relationship was based on anything more than sexual attraction. Rick would always attract other women, and what man could help but respond when the most desirable women in the world – beautiful models, sexy film stars – would be throwing themselves at him on a daily basis. Louise had already seen that he hadn't the will to resist.

Then, quite suddenly, his voice came in her ear, interrupting her reverie.

'You know Louise, sex with you is wonderful. But it's not enough.'

'Oh!'

She was stunned. Did he have to rub it in quite

so cruelly? Anger drove her to her feet. She picked up her clothes and turned from him, cheeks burning, then dashed from the room. All she wanted now was to be alone, to recover from the latest humiliation as best she could.

Once inside the spare room Louise slammed the door behind her, threw her clothes on the chair and flung herself face down on the bed where she proceeded to sob her heart out. So loudly was she weeping that it came as a complete surprise, a few seconds later, to feel Rick's arms around her, pulling her close in an embrace so strong that she found it impossible to escape. To make matters worse, his blue eyes were sparkling with glee and his mouth formed a wide grin. 'You silly, silly girl!' he murmured, kissing each of her dewy eyelids in turn.

'Stop being so patronising!'

'I'm sorry, but you just don't understand!'

He loosened his grip on her and put his arm around her shoulders instead, drawing her close. Miserably Louise sat hunched against the broad expanse of his chest. The trouble was, she understood too well!

'When I said sex wasn't enough I meant that you're more important to me than just a good lay. Look at me, Louise please!'

Reluctantly she turned her head. His eyes were pleading with her to hear him out. And behind their mute appeal was an expression that she found quite irresistible: the sweet and sensual look of total adoration.

'When I say I love you, those aren't just empty words,' he continued. 'I want all of you, heart and soul. I want us to be together forever. I want to marry you. What more can I say?'

Louise let her breath out very slowly, seduced by his adoring face and wishing, with all her heart, that she could believe his beguiling words. But somehow she couldn't, quite.

'How can I trust you?' she breathed at last.

His gaze clouded. 'Oh God, I wish I knew! All I can say is that I never want to hurt you again, and I'll go to any lengths to avoid it.' His eyes drifted away from hers and he added, in a tone of quiet anguish, 'But that's presuming you'll give me a second chance. And you're not going to, are you?'

'I want to, but. . .'

'You do?'

It broke her heart to see him hovering so transparently between hope and despair. 'Oh Rick! If only I could!'

She clung to him then, wanting so badly to believe in the dream they'd once shared. But always the spectre of Gina came between them. Was it possible for them to make a new start?

Rick got up from the bed and began pacing up and down the room. 'Look, I have to say this, so please let me finish. What happened the other night with Gina was a relic of the past and I truly believe it won't happen again. But to make sure it doesn't, I have a proposition to make. I've been thinking this through, trying desperately to find some way to win you back, and I've come up with a kind of plan. I've started doing really well here in London, getting known on the modelling circuit and all that. But people have started noticing me abroad, too.'

'Really? Well that's great!'

Louise couldn't keep the sarcasm out of her

voice. She was thinking of her own future, which she'd successfully sabotaged, thanks to Rick. What chance did she have of becoming a model now, without his backing?

He held up his hand, a pained look on his face. 'I asked you to let me finish, Lou. Please! This is my last hope!'

'Okay.'

'As I was saying, I'm getting a reputation abroad too. Specifically in Paris. In fact just yesterday I had an offer from one of the men's fashion houses to model their next collection. The trouble was, I was so fucked up over you that I said I'd have to think about it. They've probably booked someone else now.'

'I'm sorry. . .'

'That's not the point. What I'm trying to say is that I'm willing to move abroad – Paris, Milan, New York, you name it – if only you'll come with me. We could start afresh, forget the past. I know you've got a lot you want to forget too. Then I believe our love could stand a chance. What do you say?'

Louise stared at him, her heart filling up with some new combination of emotions she couldn't quite identify. Foremost amongst them, however, was the first swoop of real optimism she'd felt in ages. 'Rick! Do you really mean this?'

'I may be shooting myself in the foot here, but yes.'

Fired by a new burst of energy, Louise got up and flung herself into his arms. 'Yes, yes, why not! What have I got to lose? There's nothing for me in London any more.'

'Are you sure?'

He looked so vulnerable, so unsure. Louise

stood on tiptoe and kissed his meltingly soft lips. 'Quite certain. It's what I need, a complete change of scene. Ring those Paris people first thing in the morning. See if their offer's still open. If it is, I'll come with you.'

She hadn't felt so excited in years. A new life with Rick was just what she needed. She'd be getting away from the emotional and financial mess of her marriage, away from Gina's cynical attitudes and the temptation to slip back into her sister's lifestyle. She would learn to trust again, to love without inhibitions, to find the happiness every woman dreams of.

'Oh Louise!' he sighed, his mouth pressing more firmly onto hers. She felt the warm energy of his desire flowing through her, and soon they gravitated back onto the bed where their kisses and caresses became more ardent. Rick's legs entwined with hers, the warm bundle of his sex falling between her thighs, and his right hand began caressing her breast, evoking faint echoes of their earlier passion. She looked down at his face and saw in his clear blue eyes no dark shadows. Only a sincere wish to make it work between them.

Even so he whispered, with a rueful smile, 'You know, my love, there are no guarantees.'

'Who needs guarantees? They're not worth the paper they're written on,' she said, thinking of her impending divorce. Then she grinned wickedly. 'Anyway, relationships can be judged by more than one yardstick.'

At which the yardstick in question began to stir into action.